W9-DFX-439

DATE DUE

MAR 17 2006 *LD*		
MAR 22 2006	5/16/17	*111*
APR 05 2006		
APR 21 2006		
JUN 06 2008		
AUG 22 2012		
OCT 06 2012		

F
MAR   Marr, Patt
         Man of her dreams

Man of
Her Dreams

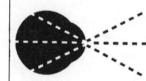

This Large Print Book carries the
Seal of Approval of N.A.V.H.

Man of Her Dreams

Patt Marr

Thorndike Press • Waterville, Maine

Copyright © 2005 by Patt Marr

Published in 2005 by arrangement with Harlequin Books S.A.

Thorndike Press® Large Print Christian Romance.

The tree indicium is a trademark of Thorndike Press.

The text of this Large Print edition is unabridged.
Other aspects of the book may vary from the original edition.

Set in 16 pt. Plantin by Elena Picard.

Printed in the United States on permanent paper.

Library of Congress Cataloging-in-Publication Data

Marr, Patt.
    Man of her dreams / by Patt Marr.
       p. cm. — (Thorndike Press large print Christian romance)
     ISBN 0-7862-7757-2 (lg. print : hc : alk. paper)
     1. California — Fiction.   2. Large type books.   I. Title.
II. Thorndike Press large print Christian romance series.
PS3563.A71135M36 2005
  813´.6—dc22   2005008986

Special thanks for help with this book go to Dr. Thomas Ebalo, to California EMT Chris Carlson and to emergency medical professionals everywhere who share the common desire of wanting to make a difference in this world. They surely do.

I dedicate this book to
the man of my dreams,
the man who has loved me for decades,
my husband, Dave Marr.

As the Founder/CEO of NAVH, the only national health agency solely devoted to those who, although not totally blind, have an eye disease which could lead to serious visual impairment, I am pleased to recognize Thorndike Press★ as one of the leading publishers in the large print field.

Founded in 1954 in San Francisco to prepare large print textbooks for partially seeing children, NAVH became the pioneer and standard setting agency in the preparation of large type.

Today, those publishers who meet our standards carry the prestigious "Seal of Approval" indicating high quality large print. We are delighted that Thorndike Press is one of the publishers whose titles meet these standards. We are also pleased to recognize the significant contribution Thorndike Press is making in this important and growing field.

Lorraine H. Marchi, L.H.D.
Founder/CEO
NAVH

★ Thorndike Press encompasses the following imprints: Thorndike, Wheeler, Walker and Large Print Press.

Faith is the confidence that what
we hope for is going to happen.
It is the evidence of things we cannot see.
— Hebrews 11:1

Chapter One

Paramedic Ry Brennan and his partner pushed an empty gurney toward the ambulance bay of Manhattan General, both of them eager to reach their rig and finish their shift. Ry had a plane to catch, and his partner, a cranky, competent woman named "Doc," had a secret life she wouldn't discuss.

When his two favorite ER nurses stepped squarely in their path, ready to tease, his partner muttered, "Not again! Brennan, you mess around, and I'll make you sorry."

He laughed, enjoying this part of their daily routine. "The ladies just want to wish us a happy New Year, Doc," he said, keeping her pace. Why irritate her more than usual? Hopefully, the nurses would move before Doc ran them down.

And they did. Parting, they walked beside the gurney. The taller one, Tonya, tossed a toffee-colored curl over her shoulder and said, "Look at him, Rachel. With that laid-back air and easygoin' smile, doesn't Ry Brennan just take your breath away?"

"Oh, brother," Doc muttered with a long-suffering sigh.

"You gotta love a guy who's all that and doesn't seem to know it," Rachel agreed, her dark eyes full of fun.

"Doc, how long do you think a man has to work out to get muscles like that?" Tonya asked, joking.

"Less time than you spend curling that pretty hair."

Ry had to laugh. That was Doc, in for a zinger every chance she got. It was just silly talk, a balance for the misery and pain they saw in their work every day.

"Doc, you know this man better than most. Do you think there's the slightest possibility that our guy Ry doesn't have a New Year's Eve date tonight?"

The silly way Tonya rhymed his name put a ghost of a smile on his partner's face. *Way to go, Tonya.* She deserved a gold star. Doc could use a whole load of smiles. It bothered him how she seemed to hate life.

"Yeah, Doc, help us out here," Rachel said earnestly. "Don't you think Ry would like the company of a pair of love goddesses to ring in the new year?"

"Don't know. Don't care." Doc shoved the gurney on, not breaking pace.

He grinned at the nurses. They'd asked for that. Doc cared about her patients, but not much else. He and Doc had an unspoken rule. He didn't talk about his love life — the quantity and quality of which was greatly exaggerated — and she didn't talk about her life at all.

"Ladies, I'd love to celebrate with you," he said, "but I'm catching a flight home to be with my family."

"Aw, that's nice," Tonya cooed.

For once, Doc looked at him with approval.

"Where's home?" Rachel asked.

"California." No way would they get more than that. He was as secretive about his past as Doc was about her present.

"California!" Tonya said, a big grin on her face. "Why am I not surprised? I thought you looked like a surfer."

Actually, he looked like a guy who'd played quarterback in college, though he was leaner these days. "That's me, all right, hangin' ten," he said, making them laugh.

He would leave it at that. When he'd lived in California, he'd been too busy to surf even if the beach was close by. He'd loved his job as a pool boy, both for the money he earned to buy a forbidden motorcycle and

11

for the endless embarrassment it caused his country club parents.

"Don't do anything I wouldn't do," he called back, exiting the wide double doors. That advice left them plenty of room — or it would have until recently. Accepting the Lord as his Savior had already changed a lot in his life.

He shut the rear doors of the ambulance as Doc, without comment, took the driver's seat. The woman had a control issue about driving, but Ry didn't mind. Doc was a good driver, and he'd rather be in the back with the patients anyway.

"You're really going to California?" she asked, pulling away from the hospital.

"Do you think I'd make that up to get out of a date?"

"I never know what you'll do."

"Aw, Doc. I never lie."

She snorted skeptically but didn't argue. How could she? Even before he'd become a Christian, he'd been a stickler for the truth. There were times when patients might think he was more optimistic about their condition than he actually was, but that was for their benefit. It made them easier to treat when they were calm.

"When are you coming back?" she asked, scowling.

"How sweet of you to ask. I knew you cared," he teased. That's the way it was between them. He let her be as grumpy as she wanted. She gave him room to have fun. It made the shift pass.

She sighed heavily. "If I'm going to have to break in a new partner, I'd like some time to get used to the idea."

He smiled to himself. That was Doc's way of saying she'd miss him. Well, not him, but the change in her routine. "No need to fret, Doc. I'll be back after our forty-eight hours off. I couldn't live without you."

"Yeah, right. You've got time coming. Take it."

He'd thought about it. The trip was a lot of money and travel for a couple of nights, yet even that might be too long. His fuse could be pretty short when it came to his family. If he didn't feel so strongly about starting the new year off right, he wouldn't be going home. Unless this visit went as he prayed it would, he would never go back.

Meg Maguire slid the clothes hangers from one end of her closet to the other, searching for something that would do for the Brennans' New Year's Eve party. There were plenty of bridesmaid dresses, but nobody wore those, no matter what the bride said about choosing a dress that would work for other occasions.

What other occasions? Meg's job required jeans and pants in the basic colors, some tops and a few jackets. For social occasions, she added shorts. That was it. If there was a pair of panty hose in her chest of drawers, it would be a miracle, and any dressy shoes in those boxes on the top shelf would have partnered one of the bridesmaid dresses.

She should have gone shopping, but she would rather clean the grout in her shower than shop. It wasn't that she was so hard to please. Just the opposite, she liked a lot of colors and styles. There were plenty of size fours that fit. It was the multitude of choices that made her crazy. As often as not, she came home empty-handed.

The Brennans' party was definitely a dress-up affair, or it used to be in the days when she'd been best friends with Beth and Ry. When they were little, they'd spied on the guests, laughed at them in their party hats and had more fun than anyone.

She glanced at the bedside picture of the three of them taken at Disneyland when she and Beth had been toothless six-year-olds and Ry was only a couple of years older. There was such pure joy in their young faces that she loved that photo.

She'd been so lucky to have them as her unofficial sister and brother. Adopted into her heart, she'd loved them as surely as she loved her older brother, Pete, who had been their faithful rescuer, while *their* older brother, Trey, had been their worst enemy. A born tattletale, he'd practically forced Beth and Ry to hang out at the Maguires'.

Down the hill from the Brennans', the Maguire family had a big yard where kids gathered to play. Inside the house was a filled cookie jar and a refrigerator stocked with cold drinks. Meg's mom was always home, though usually busy in her studio, sculpting the art pieces that made her famous. Meg's dad sometimes stopped by during the day and was home every night from his job as a general contractor. He joked with the kids, often played with them and treated the Brennans as if they were his.

At the Brennans' house, it was a totally different atmosphere. Meg hated to go there. Their professionally landscaped grounds won Garden Club prizes, but they weren't designed for kids to enjoy. The whole house was kid-*un*friendly. TV and electronic games were not allowed, and the maid had to enforce Mrs. Brennan's no-snacks rule if she wanted to keep her job. If she gave the kids a break, Trey invariably told.

Trey — Dr. James Thomas Brennan III. Just the thought of him made Meg's stomach churn. He'd been a snooty, bratty kid, and he'd become an arrogant, unlikeable man with an arrogant, unlikeable wife.

Maybe she was wrong, but Meg still blamed Trey for Ry leaving the way he did, though Deborah Brennan might be more to blame. The pressure his mother put on Ry would have turned any good kid into a rebel who chose to go his own way, no matter the cost.

Meg hated the idea of having to be civil to that woman and to the other Brennan men — Trey, his dad, his granddad and his uncles — all of them medical doctors who looked down on Ry for breaking free. She was glad he had, and sad for Beth who hadn't escaped. Sure, Beth said she liked being a doctor, but Meg had to wonder. Apart from her work, Beth had no life.

Meg plopped down on her bed and stared at the ceiling, wishing she hadn't promised Beth that she would show up tonight. For Beth, who would soon occupy an office at Brennan Medical Clinic, the party was a command performance. If Meg weren't so lonely for Beth's company, she would rather stay right here, just as she had last year, and party with a liter of diet cola, a bag of microwaved popcorn and a six-pack of Snickers.

She'd had offers for group parties as well as single dates, just none from anyone who mattered. At midnight, if she couldn't be in the arms of a man who put stars in her eyes and a forever feeling in her heart, she'd rather be alone. Like Valentine's Day, New Year's Eve was for lovers, only better because it was all about hope for tomorrow.

She glanced again at the little bedside photo of Beth, Ry and herself — three happy little kids. Where would Ry be tonight? Of course he would be with a great-looking woman. That was a given, but Meg prayed that woman would love him enough to make up for the love he'd missed, growing up.

Leave it to her to think of that. When she made her living, helping couples find each other on *Dream Date*, she naturally thought that everyone was longing for love. Ry might not be ready to settle down. On the other hand, she was so ready, it hurt.

It was a year ago tonight that she'd asked God to help her find her guy. Believing He would, she'd begun every day, fully expecting to meet Mr. Right. A year was a long time to wait. Had her prayer gone amiss, or had she missed her guy?

She checked her watch. There were still a few hours to shop. It wasn't likely that the man of her dreams would be among the Brennans' guests, but the Word said to pray and to believe. If she were going to meet Mr. Right tonight, she ought to be wearing something better than an old bridesmaid dress.

Ry eyed the lighted seat belt sign and wondered how many times the plane would circle LAX before the pilot received permission to land. His initial enthusiasm for the trip had worn off someplace over Wichita. What had seemed a great idea earlier in the day lost its appeal by the minute.

He'd done many impulsive things in his life, but the urge to make this trip could be his worst. What would he really accomplish by going home tonight?

Home. Most people seemed to think of that place with such reverence. They wouldn't if they'd been told, "You don't belong here." If there was one phrase that ought to be stricken from the English language, that was it. Deadly, powerful, hurtful to the bone, it could break a person's spirit if he stayed around.

But he'd been a kid back then, and just possibly, he'd been as wrong in his insights as his young patient this morning. The kid had been more scared of what his dad would say about the car being totaled than he was of his own injuries, and the kid had been very wrong. Ry had seen the boy's father, bent over with grief at the loss of his son.

How had the two of them got it so tangled up? Was it that way with him and his family? Had he seen things from a kid's point of view and misunderstood?

Unlike the kid, Ry had the chance to find out. For once, he would love to admit he was wrong. Make that twice. He'd been wrong to exclude God from his life. The sooner he made things right with his family, the better.

His gut instinct said he was hoping for the impossible, that he was crazy to fly straight back into trouble. For years, words like, "Why can't you be like your brother?" "As long as you live under my roof," and "You don't belong" had bounced off the walls of his mind like echoes in a deep, dark well. It had to end, and that began with forgiveness.

Tonight, as the new year began, was the perfect time to show Christ's love and prove that he wasn't the rebel his family remembered.

Ry shifted in his seat, uncomfortable at being sandwiched in the center seat for so long. When he'd started the trip, he'd had an aisle seat, but a couple came aboard wearing Bride and Groom T-shirts and discovered they were both in center seats — one beside him. A couple ought to start their honeymoon together. Before selfishness could set it, Ry was on his feet, offering his seat to the groom.

His new seatmate on the aisle was a heavyset lady who was clearly exhausted and had napped most of the way, though she wouldn't be rested, not with the apneas she'd had. He'd kept an uneasy vigil, ready to wake the poor woman if she didn't start breathing again on her own.

She stirred now and sleepily said, "Are we there?"

"Just about."

"I hope I didn't snore. My husband says I do."

Her husband was right, but why embarrass the lady? "Who would notice with the engine noise so loud?" he said.

The little guy in the window seat squirmed and said, "Ry, could we play some more?"

Early in the flight, he'd felt sorry for the bored little guy and asked what was in his backpack. If Ry had known it would lead to endless action-figure fantasies, he might not have been such a pal. But one more time, he sent a plastic hero rocketing to a new mission.

The lady beside him beamed. "You're wonderful with children," she said. "Do you have some of your own?"

He shook his head. "I'm not married." That, of course, did not preclude parenthood, but it did for him.

"You'll be a wonderful father," she claimed. It was strange how women of all ages got misty-eyed over the sight of a big guy playing with a little kid, but if there were any more Brennans, it would be up to his brother.

The youngest flight attendant, a very pretty redhead who'd stopped by a couple of extra times, stopped now to say to his little buddy, "Honey, you need to put away your toys. Stow that bag under the seat."

Ry gave her a grateful look. She returned it with a wink and slipped him a bit of paper. He'd bet their safe landing it was her phone number. Wow! She must need a New Year's Eve date pretty bad to spend it with a superhero junkie.

Unfortunately, even he had his standards. A guy ought to know the name of his New Year's Eve date without having to read it off her ID badge.

Yet it did make him smile to think of how disgusted his brother, Trey, would be if Ry brought her along on his first visit home in a decade. That made it almost worth doing.

The hum of the plane's engines changed, signaling their descent. If all went well, he would get to his parents' house before midnight and give the first New Year kiss to the woman least likely to want it. Would his mother tell him to get out again?

The metallic threads in Meg's new strapless dress chafed the tender skin of her underarms every time she moved, no matter how careful she was. She would never wear the scratchy thing again. It should have stayed on the sales rack, and she should have purchased that soft, silky thing with the high neck. No wonder she hated to shop.

But she did look good. Her image in the huge gilt mirror on the Brennans' marble foyer wall gave her a nice boost of confidence. She had taken the time with her hair, and it fell in dark curls to her bare shoulders, contrasting nicely with her silvery-white dress.

On the hanger, the dress had looked like a skirt with a stretchy band that should have gone at the waist instead of across her breasts where the clerk said it belonged. The scratchy, miserable thing did look gorgeous, skimming her body to her bare knees. She'd decided against the nuisance of panty hose, but accepted the torture of silvery sandal stilettos. Pain was worth it when shoes were this pretty.

Unfortunately, she'd gone to this trouble for nothing. Mr. Right was not here. She'd made a thorough search. Most of the guests were Beth's parents' age, and the few eligibles weren't meant for her. She wished she'd stayed home, though the Brennans' caterers had done much better than popcorn and Snickers.

She was on her second plate, tasting everything. At first it had been a problem, getting the food to her mouth without her inner arm contacting her scratchy dress, but she'd discovered a technique that worked. Holding her arm out awkwardly, she probably looked a little weird, but there was nobody here to impress, and why go home with abrasions?

It was a lovely party with the rooms aglow with candles and still-beautiful Christmas decorations. There wasn't a drop of alcohol, not even in the punch, but the party had a silliness that most people got out of a bottle.

No doubt, it was the hats. The guests circulated, wearing the most silly, elaborate party hats imaginable. The Brennans spared no expense, and everyone wore them, even Beth's dad, the great Dr. James T. Brennan, Jr. In the medical community, the man walked on water, but tonight he wore a satin sailor hat, cocked to the side, with the number of the new year flashing in gold lights on the brim.

Beth wore a red satin beret with a coiled wire toy on top. It slid from side to side as if it had a life of its own.

Meg's hat, chosen for her by Beth, was worthy of a showgirl. Tall blue plumes sprouted from a silver crown, jiggling and waving with every turn of her head.

Trey, on host duty at the front door, wore a cowboy hat with a long, spiky feather that made him look like he might be a nice guy. It was too bad he wasn't.

"What are you doing over here in the corner?"

Beth had found her. Meg wasn't surprised. Keeping tabs on each other — that's what best friends did. Or they used to before Beth went to medical school.

"Just enjoying the feel of my feathers,"

she said, swaying to the music, letting the plumes dance.

"If I know you," Beth said, "you're putting pairs together, just like you do at work."

Beth was right. "Call it an occupational hazard," Meg joked.

Beth stepped beside her and scanned the crowd from Meg's point of view. "Okay, who goes with who?"

"Sorry, I'm off duty," Meg said, swirling sauce onto a shrimp.

"You're never 'off duty.' "

"Well, I ought to be. I drive people crazy."

"You do not!" Beth said loyally. "You have a gift. Why not use it? So, tell me, who's a match?"

Anything to make Beth happy. Meg handed her plate to a passing waiter and nodded to a short middle-aged man with glasses. "See the guy pretending he's admiring the painting over the mantel?"

"That's the new cardiologist at Brennan Medical. Let me guess." Beth looked over the crowd, a big grin on her face, enjoying the game. "Got it! He gets the cute little nurse in Uncle Charlie's office."

"Dr. Cardiology isn't into 'cute.' He likes the statuesque blonde who's pretending not to notice him."

"No way!" Beth laughed. "The blonde's a foot taller!"

"But Dr. Cardiology likes the way she looks, and I'm pretty sure that she's looking for a doctor to like."

"A match made in heaven," Beth said, giggling like the girl she used to be. Meg loved the happy sound. She nudged Beth's shoulder, and Beth nudged her back, just like old times.

"You just watch," Meg insisted. "They'll get together before the night's over."

"Well, then, who gets the cute little nurse?"

"Sadly, I don't have the pool to work with that I have on *Dream Date*. I'm afraid she's unmatchable tonight."

"Like me." Beth shrugged with defeat.

"Actually, I have someone for you," Meg said, happy that she had.

"Who?" Beth scanned the crowd.

"You're missing him. Check out the Marine."

"Captain Cutie-Pie?" Beth's lip curled.

"But he's perfect for you, Beth. Tall, a genuine hunk, a great sense of humor and he speaks in complete sentences. What more could you want?"

"How about a guy less impressed with himself? You know we don't go for guys who think they're all that."

Meg frowned. "I didn't catch that."

"Why would a guy wear a uniform to a party like this if he didn't want to show off that chestful of ribbons?"

"Wrong diagnosis, Dr. Brennan. If you'll talk to the guy, you'll discover that he didn't want to wear the uniform. His mom, your dad's nurse, asked him to wear it because she's so proud of him."

"Aww, that's sweet." Beth's face softened.

"You know we go for guys who are good to their moms."

"That's true. But how come I get him and you don't?"

"Because his eyes have followed *you* for the past hour."

"Really?" Beth perked up, her brown eyes sparkling.

"But I ought to warn you. While he's been watching you, the cute little nurse has been watching him. I think she's about to make her move."

"Then I'd better stake my claim!" Beth squared her shoulders and moved into action.

Meg laughed, glad that at least one of them would have someone younger than their parents to kiss at midnight.

"Wait!" Beth said, pivoting. "Who's here for you?"

That was just like Beth. Generous, always thinking of others instead of herself.

"Nobody, but that's okay," Meg said, faking a smile. "I'm devoting myself to your uncle Charlie tonight."

Beth's eyes narrowed. "Okay, what's wrong, Meg?"

"Nothing's wrong," she protested, laughing, hoping she would make it through Beth's radar.

But Beth took her firmly by the arm and marched her through the French doors to the torch-lit deck where they were alone. "When are you going to learn you can't keep things from me?"

"It's cold out here," Meg complained, wrapping her hands around her body to ward off the chill.

"It's sixty degrees. We'll survive. What's going on?"

Confess or freeze — those were her options? "Maybe I'm just a little depressed," she admitted reluctantly.

When they were kids, Beth would have joked with her until they were both laughing, but tonight, Dr. Beth gave Meg an assessing look. "How can I help? I can listen, or I can prescribe something. What do you need?"

She tucked her arm through Meg's,

maybe for warmth, but definitely because they were closer than sisters. The love behind the offer put a lump in Meg's throat. She'd really missed Beth, but they would both miss the party if she spilled her guts now.

"Let me tell you later. We have all night to talk."

"That's true, but sum it up now," Beth demanded.

"Sum it up?" If her pushy friend wanted a short answer, Meg could provide it, though Beth wouldn't like it. "Fine. A year ago tonight, I made a deal with God."

Beth rolled her eyes.

"I know you don't believe in that, Beth, but I do. I promised God that I would stop obsessing about finding Mr. Right and trust Him to do the finding. I thought God would drop the guy right on my doorstep, but I must have prayed wrong or something. The year's over, and there's no Mr. Right."

Beth held her watch up to the light and said, "Thirty minutes to midnight. It could happen yet."

Lovely. Meg wished she'd kept her mouth shut. "Beth, I do believe God has the right guy for me."

"Good for you, hon," Beth said with an annoying edge of pity. "I know your faith is important to you."

Behind them came a familiar voice. "Hey, you two are missing the party."

They turned to see Beth's brother Ry strolling toward them with a killer smile and such easygoing confidence that Meg caught her breath. Dressed in a black leather jacket, black pants and a sweater the color of his dark blond hair, Ry was better looking than ever, and that was saying a lot.

Surprising tingles zipped through Meg's body, tingles that weren't exactly the welcome-home variety for a guy she loved like a brother. Ry Brennan was a fun-loving womanizer who'd broken hearts for as long as Meg could remember. Flirting came as naturally to him as breathing. Pure rebel, he was a terrible choice to get all tingly about.

Unfortunately, sheer reflex made her gasp.

Beth looked at her sharply, then at Ry and back again. A slow grin spread across her face. "Well, there you go," she said so softly that only Meg could hear. "Talk about an answer to prayer. My brother and my best friend. Now *that's* got to be a match made in heaven."

"You've got to be kidding," Meg whispered. When she fell in love, it would be with a guy she could count on, not a risk-taker who lived for the moment and left when he liked.

Beth laughed softly and whispered back, "It's almost enough to make me a believer. And you thought Mr. Right wasn't going to show up this year."

Chapter Two

It felt exactly as Meg had imagined love at first sight would feel. Thrilling beyond words, it was lightning-bolt dramatic and heart-pounding real and heady. She could hardly believe it was happening to her. For an instant her soul sang.

It was a very short song.

All these years, she had been so sure that she would look into the eyes of Mr. Right, feel the welcoming sting of Cupid's arrow and know her search was over. Never had it crossed her mind that the object of her attraction could be Mr. Totally Wrong.

Ry Brennan was lovable, good-looking, smart and fun to be with, but she wouldn't wish Ry on her worst enemy. Beth and she had pitied the girls who'd fallen for him. Once they'd even formed a support group for the ones he'd left behind — girls who didn't understand his idea of a long-term relationship was getting to know the girl's last name.

She watched him take Beth in his arms for a sweet, brotherly hug and knew her turn would come next. He was just Ry, she told herself, no one to get all tingly about.

He turned to her, swept her up in his arms and murmured, "Hey, Li'l Sis," close to her ear.

Li'l Sis. It had been so long since she'd heard him say that. Like ice cream under hot fudge, she melted and hugged his neck, just like a little sister would do.

"I've missed you," he said, his mouth so close she could feel his breath. Goose bumps rose on her arms.

He lifted her up and spun her around. It was only a bear hug, just a brotherly bear hug like the one he'd given Beth, though Beth surely didn't have to deal with tingles like this.

"Welcome back," she said, barely able to say anything at all, busy as she was with the butterfly troop in her stomach, flitting as if this were their one chance to dance.

"It's good to be back."

He sounded so happy that she hugged him tighter, thrilled deep inside that he was home.

Releasing her, appreciation dawned on his face. "Look who's become a babe! Li'l Sis, you're all grown up."

Well, of course. All three of them had grown up. For such a stupid statement, how could she take it as a compliment and let her heart race as if it were?

"Stay away another ten years," Beth said dryly, "and you'll notice that she's middle-aged."

Ignoring his sister, Ry kissed Meg's forehead and said, "You never call. You never write. It's been too long."

Shoving out of his arms, she wagged a scolding finger at him. "You sneak out of here in the middle of the night, go to college on the other side of the country, come home just once when I happened to be away and have the nerve to say that I never get in touch?"

He flashed that killer smile. "You missed me, right?"

She'd missed that smile. "Well . . . I am glad to see you." Her heart was pounding so hard, Ry and Beth, both medically trained, might notice.

She glanced at Beth and wished she hadn't. Beth flicked her eyes from Ry to Meg like a fan watching a tennis match. Catching Meg's eyes, Beth had the nerve to fold her hands prayerfully and look heavenward.

Okay, a joke was a joke, but if Beth kept

this up, there would be no Happy New Year for her.

"Beth, did you know that Ry was coming home?" Meg asked, prodding Beth to snap out of it.

"No, and why didn't I?" Beth demanded of her brother. "I could have met your plane."

"I didn't even know," he said, his voice deeper now than Meg remembered. His buttery baritone was totally appealing. "I only decided this afternoon."

"And you just hopped on a plane?" Meg asked. Wasn't that just like him? Ry always did exactly what he wanted, when he wanted.

"I had forty-eight hours off. I thought I'd see if there was a party hat for me."

"I think there's another one like mine," Beth said.

"We can be twins," he said, grinning.

"Since your hair is finally as short as mine, I guess we could," Beth said, touching his bare neck and her own. "This is quite a change from your long-haired pool boy days. You were always prettier than me."

"I was *never* prettier than you," Ry said, hugging his sister again. Meg loved seeing them together like that.

"Have you seen Mom and Dad?" Beth asked.

Ry shifted uncomfortably.

"You haven't." Beth answered her own question. "Ry, you haven't come all this way not to see them."

"No, I'm going to see them, but when I turned my rental car over to the valet parking guy, I caught a glimpse of Trey at the door . . ."

"And you decided to slip in from back here," Beth finished, knowingly. "Good idea. Trey's still the same. He lives to prove he's the only worthy Brennan offspring."

Ry's mouth lifted in a wicked half smile. "So that would make Trey the only one of us who hasn't grown up?"

Meg smiled. Good for Ry, taking Trey's arrogance in stride.

Beth raised her hands toward each of them, initiating their old three-way high five.

Allies, that's what they were. Buddies. Partners. Nothing to get all tingly about.

"Nice feathers, Meggy," Ry said, eyeing her headgear.

"Meg," she said, correcting him automatically. "I'm not 'Meggy' anymore."

"Oh, I don't know," he said, his eyes dancing with laughter as he looked her over approvingly. "I think you'll always be Meggy to me."

She swallowed hard, her heart racing though it shouldn't have. Ry could save that charm for someone who knew how little it meant.

"Those feathers are a perfect match to your blue eyes, Meggy."

"Meg," she corrected again, though she might as well save her breath. Ry hadn't changed. He always had to win, though he had this amazing talent for making a person not really care that he had.

He had remembered that her eyes were blue. The deck lights were bright enough for him to tell the color of her tall plumes, but not the color of her eyes. That had to have come from his memory. She shivered, unbelievably pleased at such a small thing.

Beth must have noticed the shiver, for she said, "Meg's freezing. Let's go inside. We'll get you a party hat, Ry."

Ry slid out of his jacket. "Why don't I give Meggy —"

"Meg," she corrected firmly, giving him a look that said he'd better conform or forget about a peaceful evening.

Fitting his jacket around her shoulders, he repeated, "Why don't I give *Meg* my jacket, and you get the hat, Beth?"

Meg's happy smile rewarded his effort.

"Not ready to face the music yet?" Beth

asked, teasing, yet understanding, too.

"Not just yet." Ry hated to admit it, but being here was harder than he thought it would be. On the plane, he'd been prepared. He'd even had his opening speech memorized.

One look at Trey at the front door, like a lion at the gates, had changed that. The old anger flooded his mind, and he'd thought about getting back in the rental car and going back to New York for good. If he had avoided dealing with the family this long, he could do it forever.

But seeing the girls had settled him down. He still wasn't sure he could manage to be the good son he'd flown out here to be, but he would give it his best shot. It was still minutes to midnight. There was no hurry.

"Stay put," his sister said, patting his arm. "I'll get you a hat, and you'll be just like the rest of us."

Was that what he wanted to be?

"Oh, and before I forget," she said, "you're staying at my place while you're here."

Beth made it more of an order than a request, but that was fine with him. He wanted time with his parents, but not the whole time. "How comfortable is your sofa?" He didn't really care. He could sleep on the floor.

"I thought I got the sofa tonight," Meg complained.

The three of them would be together tonight? Ry smiled at the fun they would have.

"Toss a coin or duke it out," Beth said, heading for the house. "It won't matter. We'll stay up all night."

"Say hello to the marine," Meg called after his sister.

Beth tossed a snappy military salute. "Aye, aye, sir."

Meg saluted back. "Be all you can be."

Ry laughed softly, watching his sister march inside. The girls had their military branches mixed up, but who cared? They still knew how to have fun. No matter what else happened, he'd be glad he made the trip.

"You two haven't changed," he said, bringing the lapels of his jacket closer together, the better to keep Meg warm. His Li'l Sis had become one good-looking woman. She looked fantastic in that shimmery dress.

"It feels like Beth and I have changed."

Her beautiful dark hair was still long. It was amazing how happy he was about that. Li'l Sis was adorable. She still stood all of five feet three, but she had definitely grown up.

"This is the first time Beth and I have spent together in ages," she said a bit unevenly, as if she were nervous.

He felt a little nervous himself. But it had been a long time since they'd been alone. Even old friends had to get back in their groove.

"I'll be glad when she's through with her residency."

He drew Meg under his arm. In that little dress, she could probably use the extra warmth from his body. "I only hope Beth has done this for herself. You have to want it, being a doctor and putting up with the life."

"Did you ever want to be a doctor, Ry? Just for yourself, not for the family?"

Had anyone ever asked him that? Everyone seemed to assume he'd chosen to become a paramedic instead of a doctor just to spite the family. He hadn't minded, and it was true that he didn't want to be like them.

"I like helping people," he replied, not really answering the question.

"Which you do as a paramedic."

Darling Meggy, still backing him. "Sometimes I wish I could do more." He could be honest with her. "Much more."

"As a paramedic, you must see some terrible things."

He was here because of one of those terrible things, so terrible that it finally got through to him. Pretty soon, he'd have to go inside and do what he'd come to do.

"This isn't exactly party talk, is it?" he said, not wanting to burden her with his troubles.

"I always loved our serious talks," she said softly, looking up at him so sweetly his heart skipped a beat. If she were just another pretty woman, he'd be thinking about stealing a kiss.

"If I recall, those serious talks mainly focused on your love life," he teased, getting back into their groove.

"It was never all about me!" she protested.

"Li'l Sis, life was always all about you," he said, laughing. It wasn't, but he loved to tease.

"How can you say that?" She stepped away, a move that set the feathery plumes of her crown waving madly.

"I take it back," he said, pulling her back.

She let him, but she shook a finger at him. "Ry Brennan, I spent half of my life listening to you talk about your girls. It was endless."

He feigned innocence. "You didn't want to listen?"

"Well, sure I did. I was a kid who knew nothing about dating. You taught me everything I know about boys."

"It was an awesome responsibility," he said gravely, laughing inside.

"You didn't do that great a job. What I learned was that boys can be real jerks. You'd say one girl was cute, but too sensitive. Another had great eyes, but was too flighty. Another one, you liked her big . . . chest, but she wasn't —"

"Enough!" He stopped her with a finger to her pretty lips. "Thanks for the trip down memory lane."

That would be Jani, Joanie and Sue, in that order. He never forgot a pretty face, but it would be best not to mention that at the moment. It was sufficiently embarrassing that he'd ever talked about girls that way.

"Okay, then, let's talk about the present," she said, as if she were throwing down the gauntlet. "Are you alone on this trip or do you have a babe stashed away in your car? I heard that you brought a girl to your grandmother's funeral — a girl you barely knew."

Ouch. Meg still knew how to target a weak spot. "I just brought her along for Trey's benefit."

A wicked smile of approval slid across her pretty face. "Good idea. Tattletale Trey, judge and jury for all indiscretions. He must have loved that."

He grinned back. "No more than Mom." Meg's laugh surrounded his heart. Their old camaraderie and special connection was still there.

"I'm ba-ck," Beth sang out, carrying a red satin beret like her own, complete with the springy toy on top.

"Did you check on the marine?" Meg asked, stepping away, leaving his arm empty. That was okay. He needed both hands to position his beret so the toy on top wouldn't fall off.

Beth waved a hand, dismissing the marine. "He was talking to the cute little nurse. I can wait to find true love. I'd rather be with you two."

"Beth! He was perfect for you," Meg insisted.

His sister shrugged and said directly to him, "She's usually right. Meg has a real gift for matchmaking. The marine and I could have been a match made in heaven."

"Will you get off of that?" Meg gave Beth a warning glare.

Ry chuckled to himself. He had no idea what they were talking about, but with those two, it was always something.

"Meg's in denial," his sister said, ignoring Meg's glare. "She's mad because I know her guy is perfect for her even if she won't admit it."

Meg had a boyfriend? Well, good for her. And sympathy for the guy. That dude's hope of peace and tranquillity were behind him. "Who's the lucky guy?" he said, vaguely aware that he didn't really want to know.

Meg jutted one hip to the side and planted a defiant fist on it. "There is no 'guy'! And your sister would be wise to stick to pediatrics, which we hope she knows something about."

"No guy? Or nobody inside?" He nodded toward the house, setting the toy on his hat bobbing, which made Beth smile even if Meg still had fire in her eyes. Her very pretty eyes. Gorgeous, really.

"I mean nobody anywhere," she said emphatically, her feathers bouncing.

He didn't know what she was so upset about, but egging her on was his idea of fun. "No date for New Year's Eve? Aw, that's too bad," he drawled, playing the pity card as a payback for the trip she'd taken him on down memory lane. He cocked his head sympathetically, feeling the springy toy slide.

Beth mimicked the move, setting her hat in action.

Meg caught their act and laughed. "So, where's your date, Big Talker?" she sassed.

"Who needs a date?" he said, enjoying himself more than he would have imagined. "I'm out here talking to my two favorite girls and playing with my hat."

"Ry, don't let her change the subject," Beth said, laughing. "Make her tell you about her guy."

Meg glared at Beth, her lips sealed.

"Meg, are you holding out on me?" he challenged. "We've never had secrets. Tell me about your fella."

"There is no 'guy'!" She threw up her hands. "What part of that do you not understand?"

"Oh, no," he said in mock worry. "Please tell me you're not in some secret relationship?" He knew better. Meg couldn't keep a secret if her life depended on it. "He's probably married. Never agree to a secret relationship with a man, Meggy."

"Meg! And it's nothing like that!"

He didn't believe it was. "Let me meet the guy. I'll get the truth."

She headed for the house, her feathers bouncing. "I'm leaving. Happy New Year to you both."

Beth caught up with her, took her arm and said, "That was a fast half hour, wasn't it? At thirty minutes to midnight, we thought we'd spend the rest of the year alone."

Meggy made a little choking sound.

"Are you okay?" he asked, catching up to them. It was second nature for him to check out anything that didn't sound healthy.

"I'm fine," she said, practically spitting her answer as she rushed to the house, leaving them behind.

"Ready to face the music?" his sister asked, suddenly serious.

"Ready as I'll ever be."

"Don't expect too much from Mom, Ry."

"Don't worry, sis. She can throw me out, but I'll still be glad I came."

"I'll be close by," she promised.

It was good, having her here to shore up his courage.

Inside the house, the sight of his uptight family decked out in their headgear made him laugh out loud. Most of the guests were his parents' colleagues, people who held lives in their hands every day. No one would know it to see them choosing noisemakers and trying their blow-out horns. He'd come inside at just the right moment. Amid this pandemonium, he went unnoticed.

He spotted his brother, Trey, with his arm around a woman who was probably his new wife. The two of them looked as if they could barely tolerate the bedlam. If Ry knew Trey, his brother would rather be in surgery — or having it.

There was a drumroll going, and the trumpet guy tooted a fancy fanfare. Everyone started yelling the countdown to midnight. "Five-four-three-two-one," and the band struck up "Auld Lang Syne."

And then, as if a neon sign blinked "Hug now," everyone was embracing. Why his undemonstrative family needed the license of this one moment a year to express feelings, Ry would never understand. It was enough to enjoy it.

He headed first for his mother. The way they'd left it, her greeting would gauge whether he was welcome here.

"Happy New Year, Mom," he said, taking her in his arms. She felt too thin, but that wasn't new. What was new was the startled look of love in her eyes. Whatever he'd done to merit that, he'd like to know so he could do it again.

"Ry," she said, patting his face delightedly. "You've come home! I'm so happy."

All the love he'd felt as a little boy for his mother filled his heart. "I'm happy to see

47

you, too, Mom," he said, wishing this moment could last.

She pulled his head down for a kiss on his forehead, and his knees almost buckled. When had she ever done that?

"Thank you, Mom," he managed to say. And then she was opening her arms to a guest he didn't know.

He went through the motions, hugging people he knew and people he didn't, more aware of the intense emotion he still felt than anything else. He hugged Aunt Jackie who didn't seem to recognize him, but gave him a juicy kiss on the cheek. Uncle Al shouted, "Happy New Year!" in his ear as if he were deaf, and a flamboyant blonde kissed him as if they were lovers.

Rubbing his lips to remove the blonde's lipstick, he spotted Meg making the rounds as he was and instantly felt much better. She was easy to keep track of, with the blue plumes of her party hat waving in the air. Man, she looked pretty. Her silvery-white dress showed off a figure just right for her size.

"Give us a kiss, Ry," Aunt Claire commanded, pulling him down to her level.

At least she recognized him. He aimed a kiss at her cheek, but she turned her head and planted a wet one on his lips. Oh, man!

Aunt Claire was a sweetheart, but did she have to do that?

She moved on to another victim, and he looked for a non-relative babe. Now that Aunt Claire had shown him how to kiss, he ought to practice.

He felt a touch on his arm. Behind him, Meg stood with a Happy New Year smile.

"Happy New Year, Li'l Sis." He took her in his arms for a regulation New Year's kiss, just a little smooch like he'd given to Aunt Jackie and Aunt Claire.

But the touch of Meg's soft lips on his sent awareness shooting to his brain. Again, he kissed her softly, tentatively, the way a guy did in a first kiss.

And that's what it was, not a New Year's kiss, but a genuine first kiss, the kind that had to be soft and slow and enjoyed in heart-racing pleasure. Her arms crept around his neck, and the feel of Meggy in his arms . . .

Whoa! Meggy in his arms? Shame on him. He broke the kiss, wondering how he could explain this away.

But he might not have to bother. She looked up at him with an expression that just about knocked him out. Big, blue and confused, her eyes said she'd felt the same jolt he had and didn't know what to do with it, either.

He owed it to both of them to find out. He lowered his head, eager to touch her lips again, to feel that same sweet awakening. On an unimportant level, he noticed that her dress sure was scratchy.

He heard the sound of fireworks outside and knew that people passed by them on their way to the deck. From the sound of it, there was a happy celebration with exploding Roman candles and crackling sound. But right here was all the celebration his heart could stand. This was exactly where he wanted to be and what he wanted to do, getting to know Meggy in a brand-new way . . . her lips and his, adjusting to this new touch, these new feelings.

"Hey, kids!" Uncle Charlie yelled, tapping Ry's shoulder. "You're missing the fireworks."

Not really. Not from Ry's point of view.

Meg slid her hands down his arms and pulled away, her eyes filled with awe. "Whoa!" She shook her head as if she needed the world to stop spinning.

He knew exactly how she felt. That was the best kiss of his life, which made it absolutely terrific. He could still feel the buzz.

"I can't believe it," she said softly.

Neither could he. His first resolution of

the new year was to stop calling her Li'l Sis. She would never be that or Meggy again.

"Ry, you weren't kidding. You always said you were 'the greatest kisser in the world.' "

He couldn't have said that.

" 'Practice makes perfect.' That's what you said, and, boy, were you right."

Wait a minute. This was not the reaction of a woman who'd felt the earth move the way he had. The feeling couldn't have been all that one-sided. It didn't happen that way, not in his experience.

"I've always wondered about your technique," she said, her eyes laughing at him.

Laughing at him! Another zap in the heart. Maintain, he told himself. He couldn't let her see that she'd put a knot in his ego and a bruise on his heart.

"I am truly impressed," she said, her eyes big. "You weren't exaggerating a bit when you said you were the greatest."

No way would he let her get by with this. "You know, of all my students, you've achieved what no other has."

"What's that?" Her eyes sparkled as if she enjoyed this more than the kiss.

Shame on her for that. He had to scramble if he were going to save his pride. What could he say? The truth — that's what a guy used when he came up with nothing.

"Your kissing was *so* good," he said, making it sound as if he were congratulating a little girl for coloring within the lines, "that you deserve a medal, or maybe one of those certificates of accomplishment."

Horror filled her eyes.

Man, he just couldn't catch a break. "Or we can forget the certificate," he said. Anything to change that look . . . that went right past him. Ry turned and found his brother standing behind him.

"You think she wants a medal?" Trey let there be no mistake that he'd been eavesdropping.

Hot resentment coursed through Ry's body. Trey was still the sniveling snot he'd been as a kid. That hadn't changed. Was this what Ry had come home for?

Chapter Three

"Don't you have anything better to do than listen in on a private conversation?" Ry asked, forcing himself to relax and smile when he'd rather gut-punch his brother than breathe.

"Sorry, little brother," Trey said, his sickening, self-righteous grin showing he wasn't sorry at all. "I was just waiting my turn to introduce my beautiful bride."

The petite brunette standing by Trey's side was pretty in a classy, uptight way. With her dark hair pulled back in a severe bun, she had prissy girl written all over her. Ry wouldn't have given her a second look, but she was probably perfect for Trey.

She wore a tiny black hat with a tiny mesh veil that made her look like a mobster's sexy mourner. Her dress, pulled snug over her belly, proclaimed her to be in her last trimester. Ry hoped she wouldn't mind raising the kids alone. Trey couldn't stand little kids.

"Izzie," his brother said, "this is the prodigal son — my brother, Rylander Hamilton Brennan."

Ry didn't mind the prodigal bit, but he hated being called Rylander Hamilton. That name belonged to Mom's coldhearted father.

"Just 'Ry' will do. It's good to meet you, Izzie," he said, stepping forward to greet his new sister-in-law with a brotherly hug. Any woman named Izzie had to be cool.

But she checked his move, extending her hand for a handshake. "I prefer 'Isabel,'" she said, glancing uneasily at Trey. "Only Trey calls me 'Izzie.'"

" 'Isabel' it is." The name thing again. He supposed he could understand that, even though he did wonder what she seemed so nervous about. The way Trey held her close to his side suggested Trey's old nasty jealousy, but surely Trey wouldn't think Ry would hit on his wife — or any man's wife.

"We missed you at our wedding," she said, glancing at her husband, as if she sought approval. "You should have been there, Ry."

Was there anything more endearing than a good scolding? "You write a great thank-you note, Isabel," he said to remind her that he wasn't totally bad.

54

The sterling silver coffee service had cost him a month's salary, not something he could afford on his paramedic pay. It had been worth dipping into his trust fund to do something right, which he could, thanks to Beth's suggestion that they wanted something as useless as a silver coffee service.

"Ry, I hope you won't mind that we exchanged your gift for the service Izzie really wanted," Trey said, as only he could. "I didn't mind making up the difference in cost."

By reflex, Ry slid into the laid-back mode he'd perfected as a child when he wanted to take his brother out. "Mind? Me? I'd have returned it myself. But then, I'd have used the money on something useful, like a down payment on a matching motorcycle for my bride."

Trey made that particular sound of disgust that used to make Ry's day. It still did.

"Tell me that you don't still ride a motorcycle," his long-suffering brother implored.

Excellent. It felt just as good as ever to make his brother crazy.

"As a paramedic," Trey continued, "you've surely had to scrape motorcyclists off the pavement enough times to know better."

Of course he had. They didn't call them

"donor-cycles" in the ER for nothing. Ry hadn't ridden one in years. "But there's nothing like the freedom you feel, weaving in and out of traffic, on two wheels."

"Ry?" His father's voice. Ry turned at the sound.

"Happy New Year, Dad." He reached out to shake his father's hand. It was show time. This is what he'd come home for. God willing, he planned to be a good son.

If his father were surprised to see Ry, he didn't show it. He took Ry's hand, holding the grip seconds longer than politeness required. That was a good sign.

"You're looking well, Dad," Ry said in good-manner mode, though his father didn't look well at all. Ry wasn't a doctor like half of the crowd here at the party, but he recognized a stressed-out man when he saw one.

"Have you seen your mother?" his father said, his eyes sweeping the room as if he were looking for her.

"Yes, I got my first New Year's hug from her."

The relief on his father's face was pitifully real. "Good, that's good," he said, patting Ry on the shoulder.

His father's touch was so unexpectedly moving that emotion tightened Ry's chest.

"I don't want to take you away from your guests, Dad. Maybe we can get together to-morrow and talk?"

"Would that suit your schedule better, Ry?" Trey asked sarcastically. "Personally, I don't think the prodigal son should expect a big welcome here."

Ry clenched his teeth so tight his jaw hurt. This was a nightmare.

"Let's take this to the study," his father said firmly, giving Trey a silencing glance and leading the way.

"Fine with me," Trey said, taking Isabel's arm and quickly stepping to be next in line.

Beth grabbed Meg's hand. "C'mon, we're not going to miss this."

Meg pulled back. "I don't belong."

"You belong as much as I do," Ry muttered, shoving her in front of him. He could use their support. He looked around for his mother. Shouldn't she be here, too, especially when she'd been so glad to see him?

Closing the study door, his father motioned for them to be seated. "How long are you here for, Ry?"

"I fly back the day after tomorrow."

"How long have you been here?" Trey asked, as if Ry might have squeezed in a mere obligatory visit just now.

Ry checked his watch. "Less than an

hour." It was a shame that he felt he had to justify anything to his family, but trust wouldn't be easy to win back. If he had to account for his time, that was an easy price to pay.

"You started the celebration without me?" his mother said as she swept into the room, her party tiara sparkling as if it might be real jewels.

Ry felt his heart accelerate as it used to when he was a child, knowing Mom had arrived and was now the one in charge.

When had Ry ever seen her so happy? Glancing around the room, all of them seemed to be asking the same question.

"Ry's home! You know what this means," she told them, as if they were collectively dense. Smiling at him, she sat down on the arm of his chair, wrapped her arms around his neck and locked her adoring gaze on him. "Tell them, Ry."

He would if he could. He could barely breathe with his mother's full affection squarely on him. Had it ever happened before? What would make his mother this happy, this full of joy?

Slow realization crept through his mind. "I'm not sure what you want me to say," he said, stretching the truth, dreading the explosive moment that was sure to come if he didn't come up with what his mother wanted to hear.

She stiffened in his arms. "Don't quibble, Ry. There's no in-between. You're either here to follow your destiny, or you're not."

His heart sank. It was as bad as he'd feared. He could feel the tension in the room, as if they all held their breaths, and he felt terrible about it. He'd come home to make things right, not worse.

"Mom, I don't want to disappoint you, but —"

"No!" She stood and whirled away from him, her eyes hot with anger. "Not another word. Not if you're going to disappoint me."

But wasn't that his role in this family? He'd learned that before he'd learned to read.

"Why are you here?" she demanded, her tone so unwelcome it stung.

He dropped his eyes and prayed, not sentences, not even words. Just the name of his Lord, silently, fervently.

"Deborah, why don't we go back to our guests?" his father said, taking her arm.

She shook off his hand and went to Trey, sitting on the arm of his chair as she'd sat by Ry. Trey put his arm around her protectively, gloating in her preference.

"I'm not leaving until I hear what Ry has to say." His mother leaned against her elder son.

His dad had tried. Ry had to give him that. It was more than Ry could remember his dad doing before.

"Mom, the reason I came home was to wish you and Dad Happy New Year. And I want to say that I'm sorry for —"

"Sorry?" his mother interrupted. "Sorry! That's it?"

Ry froze, speechless, staring at his mother's angry, quivering lips.

"My father would turn over in his grave if he could see the lack of dedication you have in your life." Her voice shook with emotion. "With the advantages you've had and the opportunities you've thrown away, you're a disgrace to his name! Rylander Hamilton was a healer, not a glorified taxi driver. You could have been like him. You still can!"

The injustice of her words sent adrenaline pumping through Ry's body. He wanted to rush out of the room, slam the door behind him and never come back.

But he sat, rooted in place, feeling sorrow creep through his mind, replacing that first flood of anger. In his work, he had seen sick people who couldn't distinguish reality from fantasy. His mother — with her crazy highs and lows, her swings from utter devotion to utmost derision — had to be sick. He wasn't trained to identify the problem, but the doctors sitting in this room ought to know.

One look at his dad said he did . . . and was helpless to do anything about it. What about the rest of them? Yes, Trey knew. And Beth? The sympathy in her eyes about broke his heart. Only Meg was as much in the dark as he was, but she looked as if she were ready to do battle if he gave her the nod.

He couldn't leave it like this. He'd come all this way. Maybe by tomorrow his mother's mood would improve.

Searching for words that wouldn't ignite another outburst, he said, "You have guests. I don't want to keep you from them. Mom, I told Dad that I'd like to come back tomorrow if that would be okay." He hadn't talked this way in years. Hat-in-hand polite, fearful of rejection.

"You're not spending the night here?"

Another swing? She wanted him here?

"I've already invited Ry to stay with me, Mom," his sister said, coming to his rescue.

"You only have one bedroom," his mother argued.

"Ry can sleep on the sofa."

"The sofa?" It was Beth's turn to receive the maternal glare.

"It pulls out, queen-size," Beth said, grinning in spite of the glare. Nothing ruffled Beth.

"Nonsense. Ry, you have a real bed upstairs."

This was unbelievable. Now his mother was in a tug-of-war over where he slept?

"Not your old bed, of course," Trey said, plainly delighted to enter the fray. "Mom redecorated soon after you left. The same summer, in fact."

Ry almost laughed. Did Trey think that tidbit was important? His room had been right for a boy, with its sports theme and trophies that no one cared about except the guy who earned them, and he'd left them behind.

"So, would tomorrow be okay?" he asked again, trying to keep them focused on the real deal instead of where he would sleep and the decor of his room.

"That will be fine," his father said. "Come for brunch. All of you." His gaze included Meg.

"I'm sorry," his mother said, cold as ice. "That won't do." She picked a bit of confetti off of her sleeve. "I won't be here. I'm driving Aunt Jackie back to Palm Springs. Isabel and Trey are going along."

It looked as if that were news to Isabel and Trey, but they didn't contradict her. Ry didn't blame them. They'd had enough fireworks in here.

"Why don't you wait a day to do that?" his father suggested. "Ry has come all this way, and Jackie would love to see him."

Ry's mouth almost dropped in surprise. First, that his dad seemed to care. Second, that Dad thought he could influence a decision made by Mom. That didn't happen.

"No," his mother said, moving toward the door, clearly through with the conversation. "We've made our plans. We'll stick to them. And we should get back to our guests."

She shut the door behind her, and his dad swallowed hard. Had it always been like this and he'd been too young to notice? Beth and Meg looked at each other, sharing a silent communication that he wished he were in on. He hadn't known what to expect, but he'd hoped for a lot better than this.

"Ry, let's still get together," his dad suggested as if there had been no unpleasantness. In truth, the tension in the room did seem to leave with his mother. "How about meeting me tomorrow morning after I make rounds?"

"Think you can get up that early, Ry?" Trey snickered.

"Oh, I think so," he answered, letting his drawl counter his brother's rudeness. "I'm still on New York time. When I meet Dad, it will be about the time my shift is half over."

"It must be nice that paramedics have regular hours," Isabel said.

Ry loved the way she said "paramedics," grouping them with some lower form of life.

Trey gave his wife a little hug, beaming approval. Poor Izzie, if that's what she lived for.

"I'm never sure when I'll see Trey," she added. "He works so hard, just like his father."

If Trey was like his dad, Izzie *would* be raising the kiddies alone.

"Well, then, Ry, I'll meet you at the hospital," his dad said, heading for the door.

"I'll look forward to it," he said, following.

Beth and Meg did, as well, but Isabel stopped them, saying, "Wait a minute. Trey, I think Ry should see our beautiful home. Why don't all of you come over for breakfast in a little while?"

"It really is beautiful," Beth said, mischief in her eyes. "Isabel was an interior decorator before she was married. She has wonderful taste. You'll want to see for yourself."

"I'm still an interior decorator, Beth," Isabel claimed.

"Sure, you are, baby," Trey said, shepherding her toward the door. "But we won't trouble Ry with a visit."

Isabel pouted. "I don't see why not."

"Yeah, well, Ry's like magic. Now you see him, now you don't. Don't count on your dear brother-in-law, Izzie. If he couldn't come to our wedding, he won't be coming for breakfast."

Meg cranked up the volume of the music playing in her car, praying she'd catch its soothing mood of worship. Anger still roiled in her stomach, thinking of Mrs. Brennan's explosive behavior.

When they'd been younger, she'd known Mrs. Brennan wasn't a loving mom like her own, but she hadn't seemed icicle cold or dirt mean. Tonight Mrs. Brennan's rudeness had caught Meg completely off guard.

Meg's eyes focused on the taillights of Ry's rental SUV, making sure that he didn't lose sight of Beth's Jeep on the freeway. The three of them caravanned to Beth's condo where they planned to put the awfulness behind them and have a good time.

Her first New Year's resolution was to make the rest of Ry's visit fabulously happy.

She would tease him, play along when he teased back and keep the mood full of fun, just the way he liked. A short-term resolution, she knew she could keep it, especially if she kept her head and remembered he was her old buddy and pal.

For a minute there, when they'd kissed at midnight, she'd turned into mush. What a joke on her! His soft kisses brought back the old longings she'd had as a kid when her crush on him was too big a secret to share with anyone, not even Beth.

But, not to be too hard on herself, they were very good kisses. When she had more time, she should analyze them thoroughly. Mr. Right ought to kiss like that. Maybe Ry could give him lessons.

She grinned, laughing to herself. Maybe she should tell Ry. In the old days, that would have tickled him. It wouldn't make up for the memory of that awful scene in the Brennans' study, but she wished something could.

It had just killed her, seeing his mom treat him like that. How had he taken her abuse without fighting back? Beth was a fighter, and she was herself. But not Ry. He seldom had to be. As a kid, he'd charmed his way through life.

Ry had been their peacemaker, mediating

the back-and-forth between Beth and herself, calming their storms, and so secretive about his own feelings that she sometimes wondered if she really knew him.

One thing she did know. Ry hated conflict enough to walk away from it. Look at the way he'd done that tonight. A lesser man could not have kept his cool, but Ry had. She'd always wondered what happened to cross the line of his tolerance and make him leave all those years ago. She had blamed his dad, Trey, Uncle Charlie, Uncle Al and Ry's grandfather. Tonight it seemed that it must have been his mother all along, shoving the great Rylander Hamilton in her son's face.

It was amazing how Mrs. Brennan had come up with that plan to drive Aunt Jackie to Palm Springs rather than spend time with an unfavored son. She'd made that trip up on the spot. Trey and Isabel's surprise gave that away.

Poor Isabel. What a life she would have. That flare of Trey's jealousy was amazing. Ry was an outrageous flirt, but he wouldn't be interested in Isabel. Anything that appealed to Trey was an automatic turnoff for Ry. Beth and she used to make a game of noticing that if Trey wanted a purple lollipop, Ry chose red. If Trey switched to red,

Ry switched to green. It was always like that.

She'd hated how Trey still put Ry down. Trey had such a lot going for him. Why did he have to do that?

Trey was almost as good-looking — when he wasn't looking down his nose at a person. Ry had been the standout athlete, but Trey had done okay, playing tennis and golf. Ry had tons more charm and charisma, but Trey had a good career, a beautiful home and a trophy wife. Shouldn't that be enough?

A pickup slid in between Beth's car and Ry's as their exit came up, blocking his vision of the lead car. Meg turned on her signal indicator, hoping that Ry would notice. He did and moved into the exit lane. Ry wouldn't get lost. He was too smart for that.

The three of them pulled into the spacious lot by Beth's condo, a place Beth couldn't afford on her resident's pay, but Grandma Hamilton had left trust funds to see that her grandchildren could live well.

Beth parked and waited for them by the elevator. Ry walked over to open Meg's door, offering his hand to help her out. Just the touch of his hand set off those silly tingles again. It was absurd how her body seemed to be out of touch with her brain.

"Cool car," he said, scanning her pride and joy, a white convertible with a tan top and tan leather interior. "Not particularly safe, but very cool."

"Since when were you interested in safety, Motorcycle Man?" she challenged, more aware of his nearness than she ought to be. A soft breeze on her bare shoulders made her shiver.

"You're cold," he said, shrugging out of his leather jacket. "Put this on, and don't give me any back talk."

The jacket, warm from his body, did feel good, though not quite as good as his arm would have felt. She locked and slammed the car door shut, congratulating herself on remembering the keys. That ought to prove that Ry hadn't muddled her mind.

"Did you want to take your purse in?" Ry asked, nodding toward it on the seat inside. "And the bag in the back?"

Of course she did. "Maybe I should," she said, pretending she did have a brain.

She retrieved the purse and bag, locked the car again and tried to breathe in the small space between them. He took the bag and slung the strap over his shoulder.

"Hey, you two," Beth called. "Come on up when you get tired of counting stars. I'll put the coffee on."

Ry glanced at the sky and dropped his free arm around her shoulder. "Stars," he said. "That's a bonus for the trip. You don't notice stars much in a New York winter."

The way he tucked her beside him, so casual and brotherly, was no call for the butterflies in her stomach to act up again or for her heart to race as if she were fourteen, not twice that.

But as long as she had a shoulder to lean on, she rested her head there, all the better to see those stars. "Do you like living in New York City?" she asked, proud that she could make small talk in spite of bodily chaos.

"Sure. It's home."

He snuggled her close, just a buddy thing, her mind insisted, though she shivered again.

He must have thought she was freezing, for he snuggled her closer. His chin nuzzled her forehead, a skin-to-skin move that set the butterflies spiraling.

"Ry, what are you doing?" she teased. Teasing, flirting, playing along — that was her operational mode, making this a fun trip for him to remember.

"What do you mean?" he asked innocently.

She looked up at him, checking his expression. A full grin cancelled the innocent act.

"I'm just keeping my best girl warm," he claimed, flirt that he was.

His best girl? Not likely, but she could be that for tonight. Ry was a "love the one you're with" kind of guy. Day after tomorrow, he would hop on that plane, probably find a new "best girl" among the passengers or have one waiting to drive him home from the airport. Meg would be lucky if she saw him again in another decade.

"Who's your best girl in New York?" she teased, letting him know she didn't take him seriously. "Or is there just one?"

He could get used to the way Meg felt, snuggled next to him, and he loved hearing her sass. It was getting more and more difficult to think of her as his buddy and pal. "You know me," he said, hoping his drawl would disguise the state of his mind. "It's my job to spread love around."

She looked up at him, concern in those big eyes. "But aren't you getting tired of that, Ry? Isn't there someone you'd like to settle down with?"

Him, settle down? No, thank you. He'd had all the family life he ever wanted, but he couldn't get enough of teasing Meg. "You're not applying for the job, are you?"

"Me?" her voice squeaked. "Are you crazy?"

He laughed, chalking up a point for his side. "Why not you? You've become a real babe."

"Wow, thanks," she muttered, pushing out of his arms.

"Think about it, Meg," he said, enjoying the game. "You could be my motorcycle mama, riding behind me on my Harley. What do you think?"

She whipped his jacket off and shoved it at him. "I think you're just as goofy as ever, Ry Brennan."

Maybe, but he still could push her buttons. He watched her swish away. No doubt about it. Meg had turned into a babe. Catching up with her, he said, "What's the rush?"

She jabbed the elevator button and answered, "Beth will be wondering what's happened to us."

"Did anything happen to us?" he asked, baiting her just for fun, though he felt himself hold his breath, wondering what she would say.

The question startled her. He could see that, but she recovered fast. Her blue eyes flashing, she propped one hand on her hip and said, "Ry Brennan, it is not your job to make every female on this planet fall for you. As a person who has known you since you wore my mama's high heels, I am exempt. Is that clear?"

Loud and clear. He laughed until he could scarcely catch a breath. He'd only done that once, and nobody knew it but her.

Meg congratulated herself on an excellent recovery. For a second, he'd gotten under her skin, but she'd made a good comeback. "Save that charm for silly women who don't know you like I do. Give me back my bag," she said, snatching it. "You don't deserve to carry it."

Ry laughed as if she were the funniest thing he'd ever seen. Well, great. She'd made him laugh. A New Year's resolution had never been easier to carry out.

She watched him rock back and forth on his heels, his hands in his pants pockets, looking as happy as a kid on his way to recess. What a change from the way he'd looked in his parents' study. The difference went straight to her heart.

Even if it was only for tonight, she would be Ry's "best girl." And day after tomorrow they would get on with the rest of their lives.

Chapter Four

When she opened the door to her condo, Beth had already changed into jeans and a T-shirt.

"Where's your bag?" she asked. "Or were you planning to wear a pair of my jammies?"

"No, I've got a bag. I just forgot it in the trunk."

"You might have remembered it if you weren't making trouble," Meg claimed, brushing past him.

Beth took her bag. "How can you get in trouble counting stars, Ry?" his sister said as she carried Meg's bag to the bedroom.

"Meg wouldn't help me," he said, wandering through the condo, inspecting the layout. "Nice place, Beth. You must have had Isabel decorate for you."

In unison, both women groaned. He loved the sound. This was family.

"I never know whether to pity Isabel for

being Trey's wife or congratulate her for finding exactly what she was looking for," Beth said, going to the kitchen where she measured coffee and set it to brew.

"And that would be a rich doctor who treats her like a child?" Meg said, heading for the bedroom. "I'm changing out of this scratchy dress."

That was a shame. All dressed up, Meg looked like a woman he could fall for, not the girl he used to know. He wandered into the kitchen, opened the refrigerator and scanned the contents.

"Hungry?" Beth asked, pulling out chips and salsa.

"I could eat." Actually, Ry was ravenous. He'd been too nervous to eat during his trip, and he hadn't been at his parents' house long enough to have something there. After that scene in the study, the three of them had turned in their party hats and left. No one from the family seemed to notice.

"There's a pizza in the freezer and muffins in that bakery box," Beth said.

He spotted eggs and cheese. "Mind if I make an omelet?"

"No, but don't you want to get comfy like us?"

"Maybe later. I'd rather eat."

Meg appeared in jeans and a huge pink

T-shirt that probably doubled as sleepwear. Had she always looked that pretty in pink?

"Meg, I've put a pot of coffee on," his sister said. "Do you want tea? I have peach tea and that herbal stuff you like."

Scooting onto one of the high stools at the kitchen counter, Meg ran a hand through her long dark hair and said, "If we're staying up all night, I'd better have coffee."

Ry broke eggs into a bowl. "How about an omelet?" he said, enjoying the sight of her slender fingers running through her dark, shiny hair. She scooped it up, lifting it off of her shoulders as if it were a heavy weight.

Beth leaned over his shoulder. "I think you just added some eggshell, pal."

He looked in the bowl and saw for himself what happened when a man got distracted. "You don't like a little crunch in your eggs?" he said, trying to cover his mistake. It was crazy how he couldn't get past how absolutely gorgeous Meggy had become.

Meg. She really wasn't Meggy anymore. Instead of the slightly klutzy girl who used to adore him, this very pretty woman had confidence to spare and seemed immune to the fact that she had his total attention.

He fished out the bits of shell and brought the bowl a little closer to her, the better to show off his whisking technique. Women usually liked his domestic routine.

She lifted one pretty brow. "You're really cooking?"

He was, indeed. "At the fire department, we take turns. Omelets are one of my specialties. Light, fluffy, creamy — this is going to melt in your mouth." She had a beautiful mouth, truly kissable.

"Is your skillet supposed to be smoking?"

He'd forgotten he'd turned the heat on. Usually, he worked in a smooth rhythm, getting the eggs into the pan at just the right moment, but he was definitely off his stride. "I think I'm a little jet-lagged," he said, grabbing the handle of the pan to take it off the burner.

Ow! He silently screamed. That was one hot handle.

"Let me help," his sister said, taking over, using a hot pad. "You'd better run some cold water on that hand."

He knew that. He didn't need a pediatrician telling him what to do with a minor burn.

An hour later, when he'd redeemed his reputation as a cook and hadn't made another dumb mistake, the three of them sat in front of Beth's muted TV. The girls had curled up on the sofa, and he sat in a comfortable chair with one bare foot casually crossed on a knee and one burned hand casually resting on an ice bag. He'd changed into a T-shirt and flannel pajama bottoms and settled in for the night, feeling happier than he'd been in a very long time.

"Ry, that was better than any breakfast Isabel could have made," Beth vowed. "If you ever change professions, you should be a chef."

If she knew how seriously he was considering a career change, she would be shocked. Did he have the guts to tell them what he hadn't told anyone else?

"We'd let you cook every meal if you weren't such a danger to yourself," Meg said, sassy to the core. "You know what would really make this night seem like old times?"

Those pretty blue eyes had the same old innocence that usually preceded a prank. He could hardly wait to see what she had in mind.

"Isabel invited us over," she said. "We should go."

"We are not going to TP their house," Beth said.

Ry smiled. He'd never gone with the dynamic duo when they were in their toilet paper–decorating phase. A couple of years older than them, he'd been too cool for that.

"I'll spring for the supplies," he drawled, wondering if he had the energy or the will to join them now.

"I'm so tired I'm not leaving this condo until I have to get ready for work," Beth said.

"But we've never given Trey and Isabel an official housewarming," Meg argued.

"Tattletale Trey would call the cops," Beth said. "Ry would spend the rest of his trip at the police station, and I'd miss my shift. You, on the other hand, would be so busy recruiting police officers for *Dream Date* that you wouldn't care where you were."

"I would not!" Meg swatted his sister's arm.

"Would, too. Ry, she never stops. No matter where we go, she's looking for contestants."

Getting into the fray, he said, "I know what you mean. I've seen her giving me the eye all night."

Meg gasped indignantly. "I have not!"

"Either she wants me for the show, or she wants me for her fella."

"You wish!" She threw a pillow at him hard.

He pretended that it hurt. Such silly stuff, but he felt a lump in his throat. When people had a family to laugh with, they had something that money couldn't buy.

"Meg, we can't have Ry thinking that you're interested in him," his sister said.

Meg sniffed her nose in disdain. "As if we could stop that. He thinks *all* women are interested in him."

"Hey! I've changed." He pretended to be offended.

"You look about the same to me," his sister said. "Your face has a leaner, more chiseled look, but other than that, how exactly have you changed?"

A complete answer would take all night. "Let's just say I have. We all have."

"My New Year's resolution calls for three major changes," Beth said, ticking them off on her fingers. "Finish my residency, get my name on a Brennan Medical Clinic office and lose one hundred eighty-five pounds."

Ry smiled at his sister's sense of humor. "What's the guy's name, Beth?"

She smiled back. "Luke Jordahl, my attending, who makes me feel like an idiot whenever he can. I can't wait to be away from him."

"Is he cute?" Meg asked, a knowing look in her eyes.

"Sort of, but obnoxious cancels out cute."

Ry smiled inside. Had his sister finally met her match? This guy must really be something. "Maybe I ought to have a chat with Dr. Obnoxious," he said, just to get a rise out of his sister. "I could tell him to leave you alone."

"Right. Put that on your list of things not to do. I'll fight my own battles, thank you very much," she said, laughing. "Okay, Meg, you're next."

"For what?"

Ry laughed softly. When it suited her purpose, Meg could play dumb very believably.

"Make your New Year's resolution," his sister said. "You got what you wanted last year even if it did come after you'd given up hope."

Meg glared at his sister. They always had some secret thing going on.

"All in favor of hearing Meg's resolution," Beth said, "raise your hand."

Ry raised his, joining Beth's.

"Fine," Meg said, folding her arms mutinously. "In the new year, I will . . . strive for world peace."

Beth laughed even louder than he did. "Way to go, Miss America," she said joyously.

"Try again, Meggy," he said between chuckles.

"Meg," she instantly corrected.

"I resolve to remember that. Name something else to get Beth off your back," he said, getting a swat from his sister.

"Okay, then I resolve to lose ten pounds."

From where? She had a great figure. At twenty-eight, she still looked like a coed. With her long, dark hair framing her pretty face and her eyes sleepy soft, she didn't need to change a thing.

"Meg," Beth said, "we've never kept secrets. Tell Ry what your resolution *really* is."

His sister could talk people into anything.

"I've already had a turn," Meg protested. "Pick on Ry for a while."

"I suppose that's fair." Beth looked at him expectantly.

He'd thought about this most of the day. He wanted to put Christ first in his life, make things right with his parents and work on his career change. But none of that was party talk.

"C'mon, Ry, you have to make at least one resolution before Meg shares her big resolution."

"What big resolution?" Meg protested.

"Well, you have the continuation of last

year's resolution. Ry's going to be a big help with that."

"I'm leaving," Meg said, uncurling from her comfy spot.

"Nope." Beth threw one leg over Meg's lap, foiling her escape. "C'mon, Ry. Share. This is more for Meg than it is for you. If she's going to loosen up, you've got to dig deep and share something special."

This called for creativity. "Okay, if you must know, I plan to give up women this year."

That did it. They almost laughed themselves off the sofa. It would be even funnier if they knew he hadn't really dated since he gave his heart to the Lord.

"Not all women," he qualified, still improvising. "Just blondes and brunettes. Redheads are still in."

That set them off again.

"So, the two of us would be out?" his sister clarified, wiping away tears of laughter.

"Well, yeah, but you're my sis and li'l sis." He hadn't been thinking of Meg that way tonight, but they didn't need to know that. "The truth is, I'm going to quit seeing anyone until Ms. Right comes along."

"What a coincidence," his sister said. "Meg, tell Ry about your last year's resolution."

"It was that," Meg blurted out, her big blue eyes so sweetly innocent that a sizzle of attraction went straight to his heart. "I prayed that I'd find Mr. Right."

Bless her heart, she'd prayed? That was great, and he had come along just before midnight, which definitely put him in the eligible zone. Could God have intended them for each other? It didn't seem as if Meg had even considered the possibility, but the mischief in Beth's eyes said *she* had.

"How were you planning on knowing when Mr. Right came along?" he asked, wondering why she didn't see him as a candidate.

"Do you believe in love at first sight?" she asked, as if it really mattered.

He'd never thought about it one way or the other. "I don't know. Do you?"

She nodded her head. "The trouble I have with choices? It's the only way I think I'll ever find my guy."

"Meg is the Queen of the First Date," his sister teased gently. "If a guy doesn't sweep her off her feet, he doesn't get a second chance."

"Maybe you're not having first dates with the right guys," he said, knowing that if he had a real first date with Meg, he'd have a chance.

"Meg, what you need is The List," Beth said.

Meg rolled her eyes, disagreeing.

"All the single women I know have The List," he said seriously. The list of prerequisites for Mr. Right was such a chick thing.

"Not Meg," Beth said.

"You don't?" he said in mock dismay, having more fun than he ought to.

"I don't need a list," she insisted, so close to a pout that he almost laughed.

"But Meg," he said, "a list is exactly what you need. It will keep you focused on what's best for your future. Instead of trusting in love at first sight — which could have you falling for a real jerk — you can approach this thing scientifically. Have you checked the Internet? I know a woman who said she got her list there."

"And she discussed that with you?" Beth said, laughing.

Actually, one of the women from his Bible study *had* asked his opinion about it. He'd treated her concern as seriously as she seemed to. But he shrugged and let them think what they would.

"The whole idea of having a list is just so calculating," Meg said defensively.

"Not necessarily," he said. "If the guy doesn't meet the criteria, you move on to a better prospect. It saves a lot of time."

"He's right, Meg, and you're not getting any younger," Beth said, rising. "Let me get a pen and notepad. With Ry and me to help, it'll be easy."

Meg sighed. She would rather have worn that scratchy dress all night than do this.

While they waited for Beth to return, Ry channel-surfed on the muted TV, and, for the first time tonight, Meg allowed herself the luxury of really looking at Ry.

Right on cue, the butterfly troop went berserk, responding erratically to the sight of this great-looking guy. They didn't seem to realize that Ry was her pal, her unofficial brother and treasured friend. And that's all she wanted him to be, no matter what the troop thought.

Those high cheekbones, the wide forehead and slightly hollowed cheeks with long, deep dimples were just as gorgeous as ever. His dark blond hair was much shorter than his pool boy days, but it still curled in tousled waves that most women would die for.

His teeth were still beautifully straight from the years all three of them had worn braces, and his lips still turned a little sideways when he talked, as if a smile were always ready — which was handy because Ry inevitably saw the funny side of everything.

His eyes were more gray than green, but the color wasn't the important thing. It was his intense gaze that made a person feel prettier, smarter and more interesting than she probably was. Ry invariably saw the best in a person, which was a wonderful quality and one of the reasons he'd been the most popular boy in school.

"What's first on your list?" Ry asked.

They were back to that? She wanted to make their time together a fun memory for Ry, but did she have to do this? "If I have to do this," she said, "it might be easier to say what I don't want," she said, digging deep for a good attitude.

"No problem," Beth said, drawing a line down the center of her paper. " 'What Meg Wants,' " she muttered, writing, "and 'What Meg Doesn't Want.' Okay, what's first?"

" 'Good-looking,' " Ry said. "That's one, and 'rich' will be two."

"They won't even be on my list! I'm not that shallow," Meg protested.

"You're not shallow at all," he agreed, "but they'd be on my list."

They would not. Ry would have "gorgeous" on his list, but neither he nor Beth would care about cash, not when they had money to spare.

"Well, it's not your list," his sister lectured. "We'll make one for you later. C'mon, Meg, what's one?"

Meg really hated doing this, but Beth was relentless. As much as Meg loved being with the two of them, it was exhausting, feeling Ry's eyes on her, knowing he was only assessing her "grown-up" changes while the butterflies reacted as if it were a man–woman thing.

The sooner this project was done, the better. "Number one is that my guy has to love God and go to church with me." She said that firmly just in case Beth would try to talk her out of that. Her faith and Beth's lack of it was one of the things that separated them these days.

"Excellent choice," Ry approved, his face beaming. "That would top my list, too."

Meg could not have been more shocked if Ry had confessed to hosting tea parties. Beth stared at her brother as if he had.

"Faith's become a big part of my life," he said. "I wouldn't be here tonight if it weren't for that. I need to make things right with Mom and Dad. Or at least try. On a good day, I'd even like to get along with Trey."

Meg could feel her eyes burn with tears. Ry, the rebel, the renegade, the guy you could count on to do just the opposite of what was expected, had surprised them again. This was wonderful.

Though apparently not to Beth. She tapped the notepad with her pen in irritation. "If you want, I can leave you two to talk religion."

"No, you don't," Meg said, recovering and scooting over on the sofa, the better to loop her arm around Beth's shoulder and peek at the list Beth had started. "You can't abandon us now. We've barely begun this thing."

With all of her heart, Meg wanted Beth to share her love of the Lord. Until she came around in her own time, Meg would love her as unconditionally as she could.

"What's next, Meg?" Ry asked, his voice a little raspy, as if he shared her emotions.

"I guess number one on the 'don't want' side would be that I don't want the marriage my parents had."

That seemed to surprise both Ry and Beth.

"I thought they had a great marriage," Ry said.

"I never heard either of them say a cross word to the other," Beth added.

Meg shrugged. "When did you ever hear them say much of *anything* to the other?

They lived separate lives. . . . Mom in her studio, lost in her art, and Dad, on the job, building houses from sunrise to sundown."

"But they seemed happy," Beth said.

"They were. In their way, they loved each other very much, and they gave us kids a great life, but I'm not like them. I don't want to spend my life on my own. I want a guy who'll be my best friend, who'll want to spend time with me, a guy who'll love me more than his job."

"Mom would approve of that one," Beth said, writing.

Ry frowned. "Don't put that down. Meggy, you want a guy who loves his job. For a guy, that's really important."

"That's so sexist, Ry." Beth frowned. "Women ought to love their jobs, and men ought to enjoy making a home."

Ry shook his head, still good-humored, but definitely disagreeing. "Most men aren't wired that way, Beth."

"Well, they ought to be."

"Whatever. But how's Mr. Right going to make Meg happy if *he* isn't happy?"

"I'm not unreasonable," Meg said. "I don't expect Mr. Right to shop or enjoy chick flicks."

"Good call," Ry approved, laughing softly.

"But he's got to like my company enough

to want to spend time with me."

Ry nodded, agreeing. "Just make sure that he doesn't count the time you're in the bleachers and he's on the ball diamond as 'time spent with you.' "

Beth gave her brother a low five. "It's a good thing you're here, Ry."

It was. Meg wouldn't have thought of that.

"So, we're really talking about balance," Beth said, her pen poised above the paper. "How about putting down that Meg wants a guy in a profession where he can spend time with her?"

"Mr. Right will want that, too," Ry agreed. "Who wouldn't want to spend time with a babe like Meg?"

A babe? Oh, that was nice. Half of her thrilled; the other half wanted to smack him.

"Does that work for you, Meg?" Beth asked.

She shrugged. They could do this without her.

"But I'm going to write 'not a doctor' in parentheses. You don't want a doctor, Meg. Being one, being the daughter and grand-daughter of one, I know they're never home."

"But you chose to be one," Ry said, obviously amused.

"Yes, and I'm never home."

"I can vouch for that," Meg muttered.

"So, are you saying you'll never get married?" Ry asked his sister more seriously.

"No, I'm not saying that! I want to be in love almost as much as Meg."

"Beth!" Meg shouldered her hard, protesting.

"But when I do marry," Beth continued, rubbing her shoulder, "it will probably be to another medic, someone who'll understand the life. Meg, shall I write down 'best friend who'll want to spend time with me and has a job where he can,' or just 'guy who'll devote himself to me'?"

"Either one. You might as well put down 'sensitive to my needs.'" She would be as likely to find that guy as one who would devote himself to her.

"Whoa!" Ry made a time-out signal. "You cannot put that down. We will not set Meg up for failure. He won't be Mr. Right if he's sensitive. No self-respecting male is. Better go for a good sense of humor."

"Like you, Ry?" his sister asked slyly.

He sent that killer smile Meg's way . . . a move that set the butterfly troop dancing again.

"It's important to laugh. Right, Meg?" he asked.

It was important. So was breathing, which she would like to do and could, as soon as this tingle torture thing ran its course. "Put 'good sense of humor' down, Beth," her voice so stupidly breathy that Beth laughed out loud.

Writing, Beth said, "Next, he has to have a job."

Ry nodded. "But don't we already have that? He has to have a job where he can devote himself to her."

"You're right, which eliminated a doctor," Beth said.

They really could do this without her, and she could use some more coffee. Meg started to rise.

Beth pulled her back. "Hey, we're working here."

"Well, are we talking about my list or yours?"

"You don't think Mr. Right needs a job?" Beth asked.

"Don't support the bum, Meg," Ry advised. "Make him work for his supper."

The two of them were too much for her. "Fine. Write it down, and add that he ought to have goals and a clearly defined career plan."

"Oh, that's good," Beth approved, writing furiously.

"What's that mean?" Ry asked, frowning.

Meg didn't know. She'd just thrown it in to participate. She settled back into the sofa pillows, thinking fast. "Well, I think Mr. Right would want to improve himself. He ought to have some sense of upward mobility and not be stuck in a rut." That was good, even if it was off the cuff. Too bad they weren't giving points for originality.

"So," Ry said, rising from his chair as if he needed to stretch his legs, "you want a guy who's going to make something of himself, live up to his potential, meet expectations, that kind of thing."

Meg's heart stilled. She knew how Ry felt about that kind of thing. When Trey had been set as the standard, Ry had made a point of not measuring up. Her careless words had placed them square in the middle of a minefield.

"Like Ry said before," she said brightly, determined to lead them back out, "I want my guy to be happy. And I want him to like children." Ry loved kids. She knew that.

Beth looked at her with the love best friends have for each other. "He wouldn't be Mr. Right if he didn't like kids," she agreed, setting pen to paper.

"And he has to like my friends," Meg added, keeping the ball rolling.

"I'll give him a challenge," Beth promised with a smile.

Ry walked to the window and stared into the dark.

What else could she come up with? "Beth, make sure you put down that Mr. Right has to work out." There, that was for Ry. A guy didn't get pecs like his on a paramedic run.

"And I think he should eat healthy," she added.

"Excellent." Beth scribbled fast. "He'll live longer, but we won't make him a vegan. You love a good steak."

It was true. The Maguires loved meat and potatoes.

"I don't think Mr. Right should engage in high-risk stuff." That came from Ry on the other side of the room. "If he's good husband and father material, he'll be safety-conscious."

Meg smiled at Beth. Not only was that an unexpected contribution, it was good to have Ry back in the game.

"That's rich," his sister said, "coming from Mr. Motorcycle himself."

He walked back to his chair, a half smile on his face. "That remark was for Trey's benefit. I sold my bike years ago. I drive a big, safe SUV, and I worry about women like Meg who drive little death-trap sports cars."

"Do not disrespect my car," Meg ordered. She loved her car. "It gets great mileage, and I save lots of money." Actually, she wasn't a very good saver. "Beth, put down that Mr. Right has to know how to save money."

Beth giggled. "Because you can't save a dime."

"Well, one of us should think of the future."

Beth grinned. "Good planning. Anything else?"

"I think that's it, except there must be major attraction at first sight, if not love."

"That's a given." Beth tore off the page and handed it over. "There you go. Call it a prescription for love. If you can't find Mr. Right with that, this isn't L.A."

"I won't settle for less."

"Of course not," Beth said.

"Should we pray about the list?" Ry asked.

Meg was shocked. Not only had Ry thought of praying, but he'd said it. He was probably a better Christian than she was. "Whether we call it a New Year's resolution or make it a prayer, I really do want God's choice for me," she said, reaching for Ry's and Beth's hands.

But Beth rose from the sofa. "I think I'll leave the praying to the two of you."

Meg's eyes met Ry's. Their first prayer would be that Beth would discover their Lord.

Chapter Five

Ry tiptoed into Beth's bedroom, careful not to wake his sister and Meg. If this wasn't the only way to get to the bathroom, he wouldn't be invading their privacy, although Beth had assured him he wouldn't wake her. He could believe that. When they were young, Beth could sleep through an earthquake.

But he kept his eyes forward, not even glancing their way. He wouldn't have been so careful when they were kids. Back then, he would sling either girl over his shoulder in the fireman's carry and barely notice the weight of their skinny little bodies. And there had been no thought of boy–girl attraction, nothing like he'd felt for Meg last night.

He'd almost reached the bathroom when Meg mumbled, and instinct made him turn. He wished he hadn't. Talk about a sleeping beauty. That long, dark hair splayed over the snowy white pillow was a sight he would not soon forget.

Gentleman that he was, he looked away as soon as his sleep-deprived brain allowed, though his heart pounded as if he'd carried an overweight patient down a flight of stairs.

What he needed was a long, steamy shower to clear his head. Sharp, alert, ready for anything — that's how he wanted to be when he met his dad. Another chance like this might not come along.

There was a good possibility that he might leave the meeting no closer to his dad, but he would have the satisfaction that he'd tried. Ry meant to honor his parents and turn the other cheek until they saw that he wasn't the same anger-driven son who'd left years ago.

Water pelted over his head and sluiced down his neck and shoulders, easing the tension he'd created for himself, building expectations that might be too high.

He thought of the kid yesterday, going to meet his Maker without anyone who loved him by his side. Family was important, even if Ry had denied that for a long time.

Poor kid. At least he hadn't been afraid, thanks to Ry's reassurances.

But had he been wrong to play down the seriousness of the kid's condition? If Ry were the one with only minutes to live, he'd want to know. A person ought to have the opportunity to say "I love you" one more time to . . .

The lack of a ready answer was a wrench in the gut. When had he ever said that to anyone? Not a girl. That was for sure. Not his mom or his dad. The Brennans didn't talk about their feelings.

There had been girlfriends who said he should open up, and one, Teresa the cheerleader, gave him that self-help book on putting feelings into words. It had been a good book. Just the right height to steady the leg of a secondhand table from Cathy the chiropractor.

There, he'd made a joke. That was more like it. He shut the water off and reached for a towel.

A little glob of hair gel to give his unruly hair some semblance of order, a couple of minutes to blow it dry, a quick shave, a dab of the proper toiletries and he was ready for his jeans and sweater. Into his pants pocket went his money clip, rental car keys, a scrap of paper with Meg's and Beth's cell phone numbers and a little card with his favorite Scripture, "All things work together for good unto them that love the Lord."

Father God, You know I'm counting on that.

From the moment Ry turned on the

shower, Meg had been awake and wishing she weren't. If she didn't get her full eight hours of sleep, she was headachey, crabby and a sad reflection of the Lord.

She listened to the shower and felt sorry for Ry. Since he was on New York time and had missed even more sleep, he ought to feel even more miserable than she did.

She hoped he wasn't regretting the trip. For her, it was the best New Year's Eve ever. Being with Beth and Ry again had been like turning back the clock, only better, because now she knew how precious moments with loved ones really were.

The shower wasn't running anymore, but she heard the hum of an electric razor. It was easy to imagine Ry with that razor in hand. He would tilt one side of his head toward the mirror to shave the sharp plane of his angular jaw, then reverse the move for the other side of his face before pursing his upper lip to shave the mustache and . . .

What was she doing, fantasizing about the way a guy shaved? That was just plain silly. There had to be better things to think about than that.

Like Ry's prayer last night. Undoubtedly, that was the highlight of the night. Ry had shown such spiritual maturity that she knew he must talk to God quite a lot. She'd been a Christian a couple of years longer, but she thought Ry might know the Lord better.

Maybe it was because Ry had always been so alone. Even with herself and Beth to care about him, and even though he'd had more girlfriends than he wanted and plenty of guy friends, as well, Ry hadn't been a person to let others know him inside.

He wanted people to think it was all fun and games with him, but Meg knew better. As great as it was that he'd invited the Lord into his life, she wished he could find one woman to love. She didn't like to think of Ry alone.

It was a tough decision, what Ry should do while he waited in the physicians' lounge for his father to finish rounds. If he tried to read one of the professional journals, he would surely fall asleep. The same thing would happen if he stretched out on that comfortable-looking couch. That was not the way he wanted his dad to find him.

But if he poured himself a cup of coffee and paced the room, he would make himself even more nervous than he already was.

Unless God came to his rescue.

Ry poured the coffee, amazed that once again, he'd been stupid enough to work on the options before thinking of turning to the

Lord. He'd prayed about this. The Lord would take care of it if Ry didn't try to do His job.

Sipping the coffee, he moved about the room, reading notices on the bulletin board, noting that the large plant by the window could use water and wondering why his dad was making rounds on New Year's Day. Other doctors of James T. Brennan's stature would take the day off and let a resident fill in.

Admittedly, his dad did have a great work ethic, old-school values and a high opinion of his own work that kept him from trusting others, but after what Ry had seen last night, he wondered if Dad didn't welcome a reason to get out of the house.

Why hadn't his father gotten medical treatment for Mom? Or why hadn't Trey, Beth or the uncles? All of them had to see that something was wrong.

Unless his mother was only that way when he was around. He poured the rest of his coffee down the drain and tossed the disposable cup into the trash can. Could he bear it if that was the case?

It would, of course, be better for his mother. Discard the second son and experience instant healing. Now, that would make a great medical journal article.

103

He sank down onto the sofa, kicked off his shoes and made himself comfortable. What difference would a good impression make on his dad? In the long run, it would end the same, and he could use a nap.

"Ry?"

Ry woke to the feel of his father's hand on his shoulder, shaking him gently.

"Sorry," he said, swinging his feet to the floor, instantly awake and ready for anything. It came naturally after years of long shifts and catching naps when he could.

"I'm glad you got some rest," his dad said, pouring himself a cup of coffee. "It was good of you to wait. One of my patients couldn't."

That would account for the scrubs his dad wore and the bone-weary look in his eyes. "Is your patient okay?"

"He will be."

"That's got to be a good feeling." The best thing about Ry's work was knowing he'd relieved someone's pain or actually saved a life. The worst thing was not being able to do more. It frustrated him more every year.

"Do you like your work, Ry?"

It surprised Ry that his dad would ask, though when he thought about it, it was more his mom who always implied that any calling less than an M.D. was a life wasted. His dad seldom expressed an opinion on anything.

"I like it very much," he said, proud of his work.

"Good. Excellent." His dad rolled his shoulders, stretching muscles made taut from standing in one position too long. "Ry, I want to talk to you about your mother."

Ry tensed, but he wanted that, too.

Another physician entered the room, also wearing scrubs. "Mind if I turn on the TV," the man said, turning it on as he spoke and flipping past the Rose Bowl parade to CNN where the announcer was reporting an avalanche in the Rockies. This was important news, but not to Ry, not now.

His father motioned Ry to follow him from the lounge. "Let's find a room where we can talk privately."

The waiting room for families was unoccupied. Ry followed his dad in there and took the chair offered.

"You know I'm not good with words," his father said.

"Neither am I," Ry agreed.

"I need to explain what happened last night," his father said, "or try to. I was terribly upset by your mother's behavior."

"It was my fault for showing up unexpectedly," Ry said immediately, taking the blame. He would say anything to ease the worry on his father's face.

"No, hear me out." His dad spoke firmly. "It is important to me that you know it is *not* your fault."

Ry swallowed hard. When his dad spoke that assertively, who could argue?

"If there's any fault here, it's mine," his dad continued. "In the beginning, I was caught up in my work, and it was easier to let Deborah raise you children and run our lives. She made my life very . . . convenient, and I took advantage of that. In return, I gave her free rein."

It felt so strange, hearing his father explain what Ry had experienced when he was too young to understand.

"Do you remember Deborah's parents?"

Ry nodded. He'd hated Grandpa Hamilton, but Grandma Rose had been the most loving person in his world, and her death was the greatest loss of his life. She'd made him believe that he counted.

"Rylander Hamilton was a selfish, difficult man," his father said, bitterness edging the words. "Your mother lived to please him, but she couldn't. Nobody could."

That was how Ry remembered the man.

"When Deborah wanted to give you her

father's name, I thought there was no more behind it than the same respect we had shown to my father, carrying on his name when Trey was born. Until the day she ordered you out of the house for refusing to follow her father's footsteps, I had no idea how obsessed she was about that. You were never like him, Ry. I don't know how she got the idea that you would be, and I am so sorry. I should have stood up for you then. I should have stood up a lot of times."

With his head bent, his elbows resting on his knees, his father was the picture of regret. There was no questioning the sincerity of his words. If his father had been a stranger, Ry would have put his arm around those bent shoulders and said that everything was going to be okay, but he couldn't remember ever exchanging more than a handshake with his dad.

They couldn't go back, and it did little good to rehash those terrible scenes of his teen years. Just once, though, he'd like to know why his father hadn't stood up for him.

"Did you feel the same way, Dad? Were you just as angry with me for not following in your footsteps?"

"No!" His father straightened and looked him square in the eyes. "I was proud of you for standing up for yourself. I hated it when Deborah compared you to your brother and her father. Neither of them are standards by which you should be measured. You're a better man than either of them."

The sting of tears made Ry look away. Even if he'd had the words to say how much that meant to him, the lump in his throat wouldn't have let him.

"I should have stopped it," his father muttered, standing and pacing the narrow room, "but life was easier for all of us when Deborah got her way. She was stronger than I was. She still is."

"Why didn't Mom become a doctor herself if she wanted to please Grandpa Hamilton?"

"Rylander was old-school. He wanted Deborah to *marry* a doctor, not *be* one. She was trained to be the perfect doctor's wife, which she is, most of the time."

"Dad, Mom's mood swings last night . . . What was that?"

His dad nodded grimly. "As long as she gets her way, Deborah functions more or less normally. Most of the time, she does get her way."

Ry could hardly blame his dad for that. After all, Ry had chosen to live across the country rather than oppose her.

"Years ago," his father said, "the medicine that might have controlled Deborah's 'swings' had such unpleasant side effects, she would have no part of it. There are better meds now, and she could benefit if she would cooperate, but can you imagine convincing her of that?"

Ry thought he'd have better luck convincing a drug addict that his next overdose might be his last.

"Ry," his father said, unexpectedly putting a hand on his arm, "tell me how I can make it up to you."

If Ry hadn't been seated, he would need a chair. Overwhelmed, he couldn't have stood. This was what he'd prayed for and why he made the trip. If it weren't such a Brennan taboo, he'd have broken down and wept in his father's arms.

"There's nothing to 'make up' for, Dad." It was such an insignificant, little response for the powerful emotion he was feeling, but it was all he could manage. "When I became a Christian last year, I realized I had some changing to do. It's taken me this long to conquer the old rebellion and come back to make things right."

The two of them were quite a pair, neither very good at this kind of thing, but both of them trying. His dad's grip on his arm tightened. "I'm glad you're here, son."

His dad would never know how much that meant to Ry.

"If it's not too late, I'd like to be part of your future, Ry."

Ry had to smile. "You may get to be a bigger part of my future than you imagined," he said, enjoying the moment. "Get ready to say 'I told you so,' Dad."

"I can't imagine saying that," his dad said, a hint of a smile on his lips.

"I told you I liked my work," Ry began, "and I do, but it's time to move on."

"Many paramedics do."

His dad was right. Most paramedics didn't retire from the job. The money wasn't great, but the stress was. Many of the paramedics he'd known had gone on to become cops or firefighters. Others became nurses or went into teaching, administration or sales.

"I've been praying about the next step," Ry said. "It means going back to school . . . med school."

His dad's jaw dropped as Ry expected, and then he grinned from ear to ear. "I probably shouldn't say this, but you were always more suited for the profession than Trey, or even Beth."

His dad thought that? Why had he never said so?

"But when Trey said he was going to be a doctor, I knew you'd go another way. You always did. And you weren't a boy who took advice."

Ry grimaced at the truth. "You don't think it's too late for me to go to med school?"

"Not at all, though getting admitted may take some doing. How were your college grades?"

It was Ry's turn to smile. "Better than you thought. I made dean's list every semester."

His father burst out in proud laughter. "That's not what Beth led us to believe."

It was a great feeling, making his dad proud. He probably should have done it more often. "I swore Beth to secrecy, but she knew. I've already taken the MCAT, Dad."

"And?" The apprehension in his father's voice was understandable. If the MCAT score wasn't up there, med school wouldn't be an option, and it had been a long time since Ry had been in school.

But Ry had good news about that, too. He'd done better than he could have hoped for. Even his dad seemed impressed.

"The ER chief at Manhattan General says he'll put in a good word for me at the teaching hospital there," he said.

"Is there a possibility that you could move back here, Ry? We have some good med schools in California."

His dad looked so hopeful that Ry couldn't say no right off the bat. He hadn't considered coming back to stay, but if he did, he could share his faith with his family.

"Your grandfather, your uncles and I could put in a few good words for you ourselves. And, one day, we'd love to have you aboard at the clinic."

Warning lights flashed in Ry's mind. This they had to get straight. "Thanks for the offer, Dad, but regular office hours don't appeal to me. If I become a doctor, I'll want to go with emergency medicine."

"Son, you do what you want, and I'll back you."

His dad would stand up to Mom, to Trey, the uncles and Grandpa Brennan? All of them would pressure Ry to join the clinic. Where would his dad get the courage to do what he'd never done?

At the diner across from the hospital, Meg and Beth shared one side of a booth while Ry sprawled on the other. Meg thought that Ry seemed to be in an exceptionally good mood, and no wonder, when

112

the meeting with his dad had gone so well. Ry hadn't given them details of the talk, just that his dad had explained his mom's obsession with Ry being like her dad.

When Ry reported his dad's promise to support Ry's choices and his intention to be part of Ry's future, Meg could hardly keep her mouth shut. She was furious at his father for taking too long to be a real dad.

"Did you invite Dad to join us for lunch?" Beth asked.

Ry nodded with a wry smile. "He had a tee time with his foursome."

"So much for him wanting to be part of your future," Beth said dryly. "The foursome is his family, not us."

Meg couldn't agree more. Couldn't Dr. Brennan have canceled one round of golf to spend an afternoon with the son he hadn't seen in a decade? It wasn't like Ry dropped in every day. She'd had plans herself, but she'd changed them. Nothing was more important than making Ry feel glad he'd come home.

"This will surprise you," Ry said. "Dad encouraged me to move back here."

Meg felt a jolt of pure joy. Ry back here to stay? She could only begin to imagine how wonderful that could be.

But Beth frowned. "You know that won't

make Mom any happier with you. Unless you do the whole Rylander Hamilton thing, you'll never get her approval."

"I'm not looking for Mom's approval, Beth," he said softly. "I never had it, and I sure don't need it now. I would like to see her on some meds though."

"Short of locking Mom in a padded cell, that's not going to happen," Beth said.

It wasn't in Meg to criticize there, not out loud at least, but she would burst if she stayed at the table and listened to more of this.

"Excuse me," she said. "I'm going to the rest room." That would get her away from the table. Hopefully, by the time she returned, she could exhibit peace, joy and the other Christian attributes that failed her at the moment.

Ry watched Meg until she was out of sight. Her long hair was pulled back into a high ponytail today, with little wisps that framed her face. Her red top skimmed the waist of her jeans.

"Whatcha lookin' at, Ry?" Beth teased.

He lifted his brows and smiled ruefully. "Meg is hard to ignore these days."

"And hard to please. You don't have a chance, buddy."

He shrugged, feigning modesty. "You're

probably right." But he hoped she wasn't, and, in truth, he couldn't remember when he'd been turned down. If he did move out here, Meg could throw that list away. There was enough chemistry between them to start a small fire . . . and a long, God-blessed relationship.

"So, how soon are you moving to L.A.?" his sister asked, as if it were a done deal.

"I don't know that I am."

"But we would have so much fun."

"Last night you talked like you didn't have time for fun." This lunch break was the only time she had for him today, though he understood. Her life wouldn't be her own until she was through with her residency.

"But this isn't going to last much longer," she said. "When I start my practice at Brennan Medical Clinic, things will be better. I've missed you, Ry. Please, come home."

New York was home. He'd lived his entire adult life there and felt like a native.

"I hear there's a big waiting list for paramedics at the fire departments," she said, "but you shouldn't have any trouble getting on with one of the private companies."

"Dad said he would look into that for me."

Her eyes widened. "He'd better not let Mom know."

"Can I tell you something?"

"Of course."

This was going to blow her mind. "Beth, I told Dad and I'm telling you that I'm thinking of going to med school."

"You're kidding!" She seemed far more shocked than his dad had been. "You're caving in?"

"No!" How could she think that? "I'm just sick of not being able to do more for patients, and I'd be as unhappy in any other job. I want to call the shots myself."

"But of course you do," she said dryly, knowing him.

"This stays with us. Okay?"

"Meg would love to know."

He nodded. "And I'd love to tell her, but if I'm not accepted, I'd just as soon keep that humiliation to myself."

"Why am I being so honored by your confidence?"

"I may need your help. If I do move out here, and that's a big 'if,' I'm going to need a place to live."

Beth's grin went full-blown. "Ry, leave it to me. I know a perfect place. You'll love it, and if things go like I think they will, I may have to believe in God."

Chapter Six

Meg pulled her convertible into a parking space at Beth's condo, and waited for Ry to park his rental SUV. Since they were only taking one vehicle to her brother's beach house, it would be hers, of course. Days as beautiful as this were meant to be enjoyed with the top down.

She closed her eyes for a moment and turned her face to the sun, thinking how fortunate she was to have this unexpected time with Ry. What a way to celebrate a brand-new year.

Twenty-four hours ago, she'd been dreading the Brennan party and regretting that another year had passed without finding someone to love. How sweet it was of the Lord to give her this bit of encouragement, this time of heart-racing fun. The Lord hadn't forgotten about her at all.

The butterfly troop in her stomach seemed ecstatic at the prospect of spending the rest of the day with Ry. He was one gorgeous guy. She loved how his lightweight khaki sweater circled the base of his throat and fit snugly over his chest and shoulder muscles. Whatever Ry's agenda was these days, he did not neglect working out.

The troop would love it if Ry moved back here, but they shouldn't get their hopes up. He seemed content with his life in New York and, here, he'd have to contend with his mother, Trey and the whole Brennan clan. She wouldn't blame him if he moved even farther away.

But they had today, and she would make it as much fun for him as she could.

When she realized Ry had not turned off his motor, she opened her eyes and waved him over to join her in her convertible. But Ry shook his head and motioned her over to his big black SUV.

"Hop in," he said happily, looking much more relaxed now that his meeting with his dad was over.

"Let's take my convertible," she said. "Let some breeze blow in your hair, New York City boy."

"I'm not riding in that death trap," he said lazily.

"You would disparage my car?" She loved her car, every square inch of it from its tan ragtop and leather interior to its frosted white body and shiny hubcaps. "You won't, once you drive it." She dangled the car keys in the air, taunting him. "You're not afraid of the freeways, are you, Motorcycle Man?"

Challenge in his eyes, Ry stepped decisively out of the SUV, six feet of danger, coming her way with a calculating smile. She got out of the convertible and moved toward him on her way to the passenger side. At the rear of the car, she tossed her keys high in the air.

Laughing, he caught them. "You haven't had a ride until you've ridden with an ambulance driver, babe."

"Show me what you've got, big talker." She got in the car and snapped her seat belt in place.

He drove out of the parking lot like an old man on Sunday, but when they reached three-lane traffic, he shoved on his sunglasses and picked up both speed and audacity, changing lanes like he thought he was at the Indy 500.

Show-off. Her sweet little car *would* be a death trap, the way he was driving. She helped him as much as she could, jamming her foot on the floor as if she were stomping on the brake pedal and holding the door handle in a white-knuckle grip.

But when he left the freeway and got on the highway leading to Pete's house, Ry settled into perfectly respectable go-with-the-flow-of-traffic speed and drove with such appropriate caution that she decided he was a grown-up after all.

"How was that?" he asked, raising his voice to carry over the sound of wind rushing through their hair.

"How was what?" she answered as if he hadn't scared her to death. She'd forgotten that Ry loved a dare more than most. Not much of a risk-taker herself, she'd loved that about him, but neither of them were kids anymore. On their return trip she'd be the one driving.

Sneaking a look at her chauffeur, she had to smile. He raised his face to the sun as if he were shedding a whole load of care as the wind tossed his dark blond hair.

He looked her way with one of those wide smiles that made the butterfly troop wake up and soar. She wouldn't mind if Mr. Right had a smile exactly like that. And she wouldn't mind a good, steady breath around this man.

This man? What a strange way to think of Ry, her buddy and pal.

She looked at her watch and calculated that she had nine hours before Ry's plane took off. That wasn't much time to enjoy this new feeling, but it would have to do until Mr. Right came along.

This was the life, Ry thought, enjoying the warm sun on his face, not a bit sorry he was missing a snowy day in New York City. Meg was right. Her convertible *was* the best choice. Riding along in the open air was exhilarating — a little like the feeling he used to get on his motorcycle — though he still wished Meg drove something that could take an impact and let her survive. Chalk it up to the accidents he'd seen, he'd become a cautious guy.

She was wrong though about him worrying about driving in this traffic. Compared to the years of dodging yellow taxis on the streets of New York, the relative freedom of the multilaned freeway was downright relaxing.

And it was great, having this extremely cute woman beside him. From their swing set days to the teen years when he coached her on what to do about boys like himself, she'd been his constant ally and loyal friend. She'd even understood when he'd cut her out of his life when he left home. Holding on to any part of the past had been too much to handle back then.

In the future, however, he could see the two of them as much more than friends. She could do better than him, that was for sure, but maybe God had set things in motion for both of their lonely days to end.

When Meg directed him to this highway leading to Malibu Colony, Ry was surprised. The colony was full of pricey real estate. Pete had done well for himself if he could afford a home there, or maybe the money had come from his wife. He remembered Beth telling him that Pete married the daughter of Sam Keegan, U.S. senator from California. The man was a political giant and came from old money.

At one of the more modest beachfront homes, Meg had him turn in. "This is it," she said, stowing her sunglasses. "Wait until you meet Pete's wife and kids."

Pete had always been more of a big brother to him than Trey, but would Pete be as understanding as Meg about the way Ry had neglected their friendship in those years? Pete had gone through terrible days — losing his first wife, his dad, his health and everything that mattered to him. The guy ought to slam the door in his face.

But Pete opened the door with a warm welcome, pulled him into the foyer and gave him a hug that said the silent years meant nothing at all. Ry breathed a prayer of gratitude. This was so much more than he deserved.

Pete was a decade older and showed it, though he was still the good-looking guy he'd always been. Both Pete and Meg had their Irish father's dark hair and blue eyes.

"Hey there, Shay," he heard Meg say.

Holding on to Pete's leg was a precious little guy, the spitting image of his daddy. Ry knelt down to be on the toddler's level. "Who's this big boy?" he said, looking into the Maguire blue eyes with long, dark lashes.

"This is Shay Maguire," Pete said. "Shay, give Daddy's friend a high five."

The kid packed a wallop, slamming his tiny palm into Ry's big hand, grinning with the unabashed joy of a child who has known nothing but love in his life.

"Can I pick you up, Shay?" Ry asked, instead of grabbing him up in his arms like he wanted to do.

Little Shay reached out his arms, so instantly trusting that he stole Ry's heart completely. What a great kid.

Meg always melted at the sight of a strong man holding a child. The picture of Ry and her precious nephew, looking into each other's eyes, engaged in serious man-to-little-man silent communication, was one to remember.

Pete met her eyes, nodded toward Ry, and gave him a thumbs-up that only she could see. She nodded back in total agreement. Ry Brennan was a very good man. No wonder her little-girl crush had made its way back, making her heart so soft and loving toward him that she would embarrass them both if she didn't take care.

"Pete, this place is great," Ry said, taking in the nautical navy-and-white theme of the entryway.

"Thank you," Pete said humbly. "My dad and I built it for a retired Navy admiral."

Meg wondered if Pete would mention that it was the last project he'd worked on before their dad died.

Looking her way, Pete added, "It was my personal hideaway until Meg dragged me out of here and tricked me into going on her TV show."

"Where you met Sunny," she added defensively. Yes, she'd used a little trickery to set his life in motion, but would he never stop teasing her about it, especially when it had turned out so well? "You know that's when your life really began, Petey."

"She's right," her brother said, dropping his arm around her shoulder. "It's lucky for you that you live in New York, Ry, or

Matchmaker Meg would have you on *Dream Date* and walking down the aisle before you knew it."

"Actually, I'm thinking about moving back here," Ry said looking directly her way with a gleam in his eye. That gleam used to signal that he'd set his sights on a babe target. She didn't know what it meant these days, but it took her breath away.

Shay's exploring little fingers reached up and tweaked Ry's nose, hard enough to make him say, "Ow."

Way to go, Shay. That checked the potency of Ry's babe-magnet appeal.

"What's this, big guy?" Ry tried to interest Shay in the polished oak captain's wheel mounted on the foyer wall.

"I mounted that wheel for the admiral," Pete said, "and set that big brass bell into the plastered alcove. Sunny and I decided to keep them there to remind ourselves that the Lord is the captain of our ship."

"You're Christians, too?" Ry beamed. "That's terrific. I turned things over to the Lord at a home Bible study. How about you?"

"Actually, Sunny pushed me in the right direction and got me going to her church before we were married. Not long after that, Meg joined us."

"Our church is a big part of our lives," Meg added.

Pete nodded. "Meg serves on the audio-video committee. Sunny was a high school teacher and coach before she chose to stay home with the little ones, but she works with our church youth, and I'm on the building commission."

"That's a natural ministry for you," Ry said. "Beth told me you'd become a developer and that you named your first project Sunny Valley for your wife."

Pete nodded proudly. "I'd like you to see it."

"Shay, where's your mommy and baby sister?" Meg said, eager to hold a little one herself.

Shay pointed to the deck, and Pete led the way past a big-screen TV showing one of the Bowl games. To their credit, both men only paused to catch the end of one play. Knowing them, it could have been longer, even with a darling baby to see. They'd both played football in high school and Ry had been good enough to earn a college scholarship.

At the end of the room were floor-to-ceiling windows and a sliding door that led to the deck and a truly beautiful view. Shades of blue and green where ocean met sky formed a backdrop for vibrant-colored flowers potted in bright Mexican pottery.

Close to the house, under an awning, Meg's beautiful red-haired sister-in-law slept on a chaise. Baby Megan's little face nestled against her mother's neck, her lighter red hair blending with her mother's. Meg shaded her eyes from the sun's glare and let the scene sweep her into peace and serenity.

"Sunny," Pete said softly, kissing his wife's forehead.

"Don't wake her," Ry whispered.

"She asked me to," Pete replied.

"And he always does what I ask," Sunny said, coming awake with a smile that matched her name. "Want to hold her?" she asked Meg, lifting the baby toward her.

That was like asking if a child wanted Christmas. Meg cradled the baby in her arms and showed her to Ry. "Ry, meet Megan Maguire. This little girl is the new Meggy."

The baby opened her sleepy blue eyes.

"Hey, Meggy." Ry touched the baby's hand and smiled when she instinctively wrapped her tiny fingers around one of his. "Don't they get the two of you confused?" he teased.

Meg scowled at him. "I'm not Meggy anymore."

"You'll adjust," Pete said sympathetically. "We all have. Sis convinced us that she couldn't climb the corporate ladder unless she was Meg Maguire, power woman."

"And she's right," Sunny said, ever supportive.

Meg had bonded with Sunny as soon as she came into Pete's life. Now, the two of them were as close as real sisters. Their friendship helped fill the void while Beth finished med school and did her residency.

Staying in the shade, Meg strolled the width of the deck, swaying slowly, putting the baby back to sleep. The familiar rush of wanting her own baby swept through her body with its usual powerful presence.

She really did have to find Mr. Right. If a guy asked her out and met The List prerequuisites, she would give him a chance, whether she felt any chemistry or not. Maybe love *could* grow if she gave it a chance. Her guy could be just around the corner.

That's how it had been for Pete and Sunny. Neither expected to fall in love when they went on *Dream Date*, and they didn't fall in love at first sight. But look at them now, perfect for each other.

Sunny was asking Ry about their childhood — the four of them, Pete and Meg, Ry and Beth. Ry admitted he'd been a handful, and sometimes his intentions had been better than his deeds, like the time when Meg was so sick with chicken pox.

He'd only wanted to cheer her up when he fixed the nicest present he could think of — his favorite frog in a pretty box with a bow. If Ry had been the sick one, he'd have loved to have Froggie's company. But Meg had opened the box and been so scared when Froggie jumped out that she tried to beat him with the lid of the box until the bow fell off.

Ending his tale, Ry looked at her reproachfully. "Poor Froggie," he said.

"Poor Meg," she said, defending herself. "I still hate surprises."

"Auntie hurt the frog?" little Shay asked worriedly.

"No, honey," she said, reassuring the child and glaring at Ry. "Auntie had a fever and a very bad aim."

Pete served cold drinks and added his own memories — the time she nailed her shirt to the roof when she was determined to prove her worth as a builder so her father's pickup would read Maguire And Family instead of Maguire And Son. And there was the time Pete had to rescue her and Beth from the tree house. Trey had stolen the ladder and left them up there for hours.

Shay played quietly at their feet, putting colorful plastic tile blocks together. Ry motioned to him and said, "He's a builder just like his grandpa. Pete, I loved your dad. He was the only father in the neighborhood that played with us."

Meg blinked away tears, still missing her dad.

"No wonder we all hung out at your house," Ry added.

"No wonder we had the worst lawn in the neighborhood," Pete said, laughing softly. "But neither Dad or Mom cared, not as long as the kids were happy."

It was true. Their parents had their separate careers and not much in common, but there had been love to spare at their house.

"What's your mother doing these days?" Ry asked.

Pete answered. "She sold the house after Dad died, moved to Taos, New Mexico, and became part of the art community there. We hated to see her leave, but Mom needed a fresh start."

"She can sculpt to her heart's content without interruption and do exactly as she pleases," Meg added, happy for her mom. "She's doing the best work of her life."

"But you still get together?" Ry asked, as if he couldn't bear hearing that they didn't.

"Sure we do," Sunny said. "Mom was just here for Christmas, and she came and stayed with us when Meggy was born. She's been more of a mother to me than my own."

"What about your family, Sunny?" Ry asked.

He didn't know that he'd just walked into a land mine, but Meg knew. How would they explain Sunny's unfortunate family situation?

Before Sunny could answer, Pete stood up and stretched, yawning so contagiously that Meg felt a yawn coming on herself. "Shay, how about taking your dad upstairs for a nap? Could you do that, son? Your sister kept us up last night."

Shay pushed his building tiles to one side, tidy little perfectionist that he was, and reached for his dad's hand. "C'mon, Dad-dee! You sleepy boy."

"Won't we be glad when Baby Meggy learns to sleep through the night like a big girl?" Pete said, letting Shay pull him along. "Ry, help yourself to a T-shirt, swim trunks, whatever you need. Meg knows where they are."

Sunny rose from the chaise and reached

for the baby. Smiling, she said, "Mommy's sleepy, too. When they're this age, Ry, you sleep every time they do. We'll take a family nap and leave you two to enjoy the beach."

Ry watched his hosts climb the stairwell to the loft over the living room with a puzzled look on his face. "What just happened here? Was it something I said or were they really that sleepy?"

"Both, I imagine," Meg replied, opening the lid of a bench that doubled as storage for beach towels and swimwear. "We don't talk about it, but Sunny's mother makes yours look like Mother of the Year, and Sunny's father has Alzheimer's. He hasn't known Sunny for more than a year."

"I didn't mean to pry," he said, obviously worried.

"They know you didn't. Don't blame yourself for having the good manners to inquire about your hosts' family."

He still looked worried.

"Really, it's fine," she said, touching his arm.

He glanced at her hand and then met her eyes as if he needed her reassurance.

She smiled, willing him to see how much she admired the man he'd become.

He held her gaze until the butterfly troop started their crazy routine. She had to look away, lest the troop get the wrong idea.

"Here," she said, motioning to the storage bench. "Take your pick."

He chose a bright orange towel centered with a dark-haired mermaid wearing bright pink scales. "This looks like you, Power Woman, and I believe this one's mine." His choice was a friendly porpoise on a sea-blue background.

"That's you, all right, ready to chat up the girl fish."

"Hey," he protested, his voice low and so appealing that the butterfly troop did an encore. "I've reformed."

"How much does a bad boy ever reform?" she teased.

"A lot when he wants to." Completely serious, Ry's eyes met hers again and stayed there until she had to break the connection or melt where she stood.

"You can change in the bathroom at the end of the kitchen," she said, eager for a chance to regroup. "I'll change upstairs."

Ry watched her zip up the stairs and wondered how he could convince her that he wasn't the same guy she used to know. He couldn't claim the credit, for it was God working in him, just as the Word said. He didn't doubt that she loved the Lord, but loving meant trusting. Why couldn't she relax and trust that this chemistry between them would take its own course?

He changed into a pair of dark swim trunks, tossed a T-shirt over one shoulder, left his clothes in a hall closet and walked outside. He might as well catch the mid-afternoon rays while he had a chance, though he would burn rather than tan if he weren't careful.

Careful, he repeated, smiling to himself. If Meg were here, he could have said that out loud. Wasn't that proof that the maverick who acted before he thought was long gone? In his place was a responsible guy who thought about skin cancer, vehicle safety and what might happen if the Lord meant for the two of them to be together.

An inviting cushioned chaise lay flat in the sun, just calling his name. Laying facedown, he stretched his arms over his head and enjoyed the winter pleasure of warm sunshine.

Lulled by the rhythmic ebb and flow of the tide, he drifted into nothingness and dreamed of a dark-haired mermaid who swam by his side down deep in the sea.

Icy-cold goo hit his back and brought him back to the surface. In one quick move he twisted to face his tormentor and caught Meg's wrist.

"It's only sunscreen," she said, laughing at him.

He loved the sound of that low, rich laughter. Gone was the cute ponytail which he'd liked, but her dark hair now rested on one shoulder, gleaming in the sunlight. Had she brushed it extra pretty for him, and had she applied that fresh glossy lip color so he would notice she had the most beautiful lips he'd ever seen? He hoped so because that would mean he might have a chance.

"Thanks for thinking of the sunscreen," he said as matter-of-factly as he could, considering the pick-up of his heart rate. He resumed his belly-down position. "I expect I could use a lot of that stuff."

"We don't want you to get burned," she said with a smile in her voice, scooching him over so that she'd have room to sit beside him.

That was fine with him, especially if she planned to do a thorough job with that sunscreen.

Even though he expected the feel of her hands, her first touch made him tense so obviously that she laughed.

"Kind of flinchy, aren't you?" she teased.

"Kind of what?" He hadn't heard that one before.

"Flinchy. That's what my grandpa used to

call it when a person had the twitches."

"I do not have the twitches."

"No?" She drizzled more cold lotion on his back.

Of course, he flinched again. "You've become a cruel woman, Meg."

That rich laughter again. He loved it.

"I can still throw you in the ocean," he warned.

"If you can catch me."

He thought he might be up to that challenge. Her hands glided over his skin, smoothing the lotion over his arms and shoulders until he was putty in her hands. Right now, he couldn't win a race with baby Meggy.

"What's this, Ry?" She circled the round design of the tattoo on his back. "It looks just like . . ."

He waited for her to figure it out.

"Ry, isn't this just like the medallion you used to wear on a chain? The one your Grandma Rose gave you?"

Wordlessly, he nodded. Would she think its symbolism overly sentimental or would she understand? He'd had the tattoo for a decade, but Meg was the first to see it who had also seen the original.

"But the initials aren't the same," she murmured, her hands stilled as if the design required her whole concentration. "MRH? Your medallion had your initials, RHB for Rylander Hamilton Brennan."

If Grandma Rose hadn't given him the medallion already engraved with his initials, Ry would never have worn it, not when that set of letters represented a man as cold and hateful as Grandma Rose had been loving and kind.

Grandma Rose had reached high to place the chain over his long curly hair. She'd straightened the silver disk on his chest and said, "That's for Grandma's good boy."

If people only knew how much praise meant to a kid, especially one as starved for it as he'd been, they would shower a child with good words.

He rose to a sitting position beside Meg, picked up the bottle of lotion, squirted some in his palm and smoothed it over his face, throat and chest.

"So are you going to explain, or not?" Meg asked.

He looked at her, wondering what he would do if she laughed at his story. For starters, he would throw her in the ocean, but then what? Still, if he couldn't trust Meg, who could he trust?

"When Grandma Rose died, I'd been away a year or so. In that time, I'd only called her twice. This was a woman who'd shown me nothing but love, and I cut her off just like I cut the rest of you off. I must have thought I had all the time in the world to show her I cared. When I realized what a mistake I'd made, it was awful."

"You were young," Meg said, nudging his shoulder with hers, a comforting gesture. "Kids take the future for granted. Your grandmother knew how things were for you."

He hoped she was right. "I flew home, all torn up inside, trying to think of a gesture that was worthy of Grandma. Flowers weren't enough, and I don't write poetry or anything like that. But I passed a tattoo parlor and thought about having the medallion duplicated on my back, under my left shoulder blade, right behind my heart — or where I thought the heart was at the time." He smiled at his own youthful thinking and looked at her, expecting her to be smiling, too.

But there were tears in her eyes. "That was a sweet thing to do, Ry. Your grandmother would have loved it."

He'd always hoped so. "I had her initials tattooed on my back medallion — MRH for Marsha Rose Hamilton — so I'd always have her with me, and I dropped my chain and the medallion with my initials in her casket."

"So you would always be with her," Meg finished.

He nodded, grateful that she understood.

She laced her fingers through his, a gesture just as precious as his sentimental soul could take.

"It was kind of crazy," he murmured.

"Do not let me hear you ever say that again."

Whoa! Power Woman could be fearsome when she wanted to be. Or maybe she knew he'd had all the sentiment he could take.

He knew just the thing to brighten the mood. "Last night you mentioned that I brought a woman to Grandma's funeral? Remember?"

"I think everyone remembers, Ry," she said dryly.

Okay, so he'd made some bad choices back then. "Want to know who she was?" he asked, eager to tell her.

"I'm guessing some babe you met at the tattoo parlor."

She knew him pretty well. "Close," he admitted. "She was my tattoo artist. She did the medallion."

Meg murmured, "No way."

It was the truth, not that he was all that proud of it.

"Please tell me that's how you introduced her to Trey," she said, her mouth quivering with laughter.

"I did, and she offered Trey a family discount for his own tattoo. She suggested that he have a snake like the one on her arm."

"I love it!" she hooted.

Laughter ripped from his girl, and he joined her. It was the best laugh he'd had in ages.

When she could catch her breath, he grabbed her hand and pulled her down the stairs to the beach. Scooping a bit of sand, he tossed it against her legs — her very pretty legs — and said, "You're it. Catch me if you can."

He took off toward the hard-packed sand against the water's edge. Turning to see if she followed, he realized he couldn't loaf. Those pretty legs weren't just for show. She was right behind him.

And he could hardly wait until Meg caught him.

Chapter Seven

Ry leaned against the ambulance door and stared out of the window at his beloved New York, barely noticing his partner's driving skill as they sped to a call. Had this part of the city always looked so old and winter ugly? Where was the vibrancy he'd felt during his student days at UConn when weekends in New York were such a treat? He'd known even then that this was where he wanted to live.

Tourists called the city a concrete jungle, but he loved every sky-high building, old or new, all erected with pride and hope for the future. Of the many bridges that led off the island, he seldom used them. Manhattan was New York, and New York was home.

Or it had been until yesterday, especially last night.

He'd put his foot down and told Meg she was not coming to the airport to see him off. It was too late at night. He had his rental car for transportation. But Power Woman had her way. She'd stayed with him until he had to pass airport security and head to his gate.

They hadn't talked much. It was funny how people couldn't think of much to say when one of them was leaving. She had done her best, asking what he'd be doing when he got back. And he'd done his best, trying to sound normal when all he could think of was how much he wanted to kiss her goodbye. Not just a friendly goodbye kiss, but a genuine man–woman meeting of lips, heart and soul.

But he hadn't risked it.

When had he become such a chicken? He loved a dare. He took risks every day. But he hadn't risked giving Meg a kiss to remember. That little brush of his lips on her forehead didn't count, not any more than that touch of her lips on his jaw. He could have done so much better.

Overnight, Meg had become a woman who'd dug so deeply under his skin that he could hardly concentrate on his job today.

"You're doing it again," his partner said irritably.

"What?" he answered just as irritably. He wasn't in the mood for sparring with Doc.

"Zoning out. Get your mind on your work, college boy."

He hated it when Doc called him that. Doc didn't even know he had a degree. "My mind is on my work," he muttered. "Who just intubated that last patient when you couldn't?" If he didn't hold his own with Doc, she ran right over him.

"Yeah, but you've got 'that look,' " she groused.

Oh, fine, here it came. A shift wasn't complete without some dig about him being a womanizer.

"Who is she this time?"

"What makes you think there's just one?" Okay, that fed her fantasy, but it seemed to make Doc a little less cranky to see him as a skirt-chaser — an endearing term she'd used so often it was even in his vocabulary.

"You're different today, college boy. What's her name and where did you meet her?"

"Mom. Met her in the womb," he said glumly. He wasn't in the mood to play.

"Nope. Don't think so. Try again."

Bulldog Doc. She would gnaw on this bone until she was satisfied. He'd have to get creative. "Okay, if you must know, her name is Beth, and I met her at a New Year's Eve party." That had enough truth that it

143

ought to get past Doc's radar. Doc didn't know he had a sister. They never talked about their families.

"That's not it. Get real, college boy."

"If we're going to get real, let's talk about who you were with on New Year's Eve, Doc."

"Don't change the subject."

But turnabout was fair play. "Why do we always have to talk about my life instead of yours, Doc?"

"Because I don't have a life, and yours is shallow, but fairly interesting."

High praise indeed.

"C'mon, amuse me," she said. "Who's the woman and where did you meet her?"

The choice seemed to be try out names and places until their shift ended or try the truth and see if she bought it.

"Meg. California," he said, assuming a sarcastic edge to throw her off.

She glanced his way assessingly. He looked out the window. Let her read the back of his head.

What he wouldn't give for the sight of a palm tree, even a scraggly one, or the view from Pete and Sunny's beach house. He'd seen the harbor several times today, yet he felt homesick for an ocean a continent away.

Of course it wasn't the same. Those gray

caps in the harbor were wintry cold and unfriendly. There was no beautiful beach inviting him to play, and no dark-haired beauty to chase as the tide lapped the shore.

"I thought you went to California to see your family?" she said dryly.

"I did."

And the actual reason for the trip provided a perfect opportunity for him to witness to Doc. He wanted her to see that a relationship with the Lord made life worth living. She would remember the kid they'd brought in on New Year's Eve. He could tell her how that kid's death prompted him to go home and make things right with his family.

But he'd hardly been a joyous believer today. Maybe he would save that sermon for another day. "Meg is a family friend," he said quietly, hoping Doc would leave it at that. He wasn't prepared to analyze and report on his new feelings for Meg.

An order from dispatch routed them to a new call.

Ry sat up straight and charted the information. A six-year-old male was having a severe asthma attack. Man, he hated it when a kid was involved.

He turned the siren and emergency lights on. "Step on it, Doc."

145

She already had.

Just once he'd like to see drivers get out of the way when their siren blared and their lights flashed madly. Did they think he and Doc were rushing to pick up a pizza? A child might not make it if they didn't get there in time. Little kids didn't realize how sick they were. When they crashed, it was serious.

"So you've known this Meg for a long time?" Doc asked conversationally.

Ry's adrenaline pumped and his thoughts were all about how he planned to treat the child. But Doc operated best when she pretended there was no upcoming trauma.

"Since we were little kids," he said for her sake, not because he was interested in conversation just now.

"You've never talked about her or your family."

He hadn't talked about a lot of things. It was easier to let Doc and others think he had the depth of a teacup than to invite questions he had no answers for.

"So, where in California? And what's your family like?"

Good grief. Like it mattered? "Beverly Hills," he snapped. "And they're all M.D.s."

"They're all M.D.s, and you're a paramedic?" Her voice rose.

He shouldn't have told her.

"So what happened to you? Flunk out, college boy?"

If she hadn't called him that again, he could have kept his cool, but he snapped. "No, Doc, I graduated with honors the same year I led the conference in touchdowns." What difference did it make if he told her? She probably wouldn't believe it. "Over there, that's the address."

He was out of the bus before she could turn off the motor. Grabbing their stuff, he headed inside, praying that someone had been smart enough to summon the elevator and had it waiting for them. Hopefully, it worked in this old building, and they wouldn't have to deal with the stairs.

Doc backed the ambulance out of the bay at Manhattan General, noting that her partner seemed as exhausted as she was. It had been a very physical shift, and this last call had zapped both of them. How could people live on the tenth floor of a building with a broken elevator?

If it hadn't been for Ry's strength, their little asthma patient wouldn't have made it. Ry had beaten her up the stairs, got a line going, scooped up the child and met her on the way down.

147

"You saved that kid, Ry."

He shrugged as if he were angry. "It was too close of a call. That family needs a baby-sitter with a brain. They need better housing, better jobs, medicine for the kid —" He stopped midsentence and folded his arms in frustration.

This was not like Ry at all. They dealt with calls that bad all the time. Ry was different today, and it worried her. Where was the irrepressible flirt, the eternal optimist, the man who lifted her spirits every day?

"We do what we can, Ry." She so seldom had to be the positive one that she hardly knew how.

"It isn't enough."

"Nothing's enough, but we do what we can."

He made a sound of disgust. "I'm sick of it. I ought to know more, be able to do more."

She hadn't known he felt that way. She did herself, but she was doing something about it. Why didn't he? He said he had a college degree, that he'd graduated with honors. She believed him. Ry was a sharp guy. She wished she had his gift for remembering things.

"If you want to do more," she said, "quit your whining and do it. Use that degree. Go

148

to med school. Become an M.D. like the rest of your family."

He didn't answer, which was unlike him. Ry always had an answer.

"What's holding you back?" she said. "The fact that you might actually have to work a little?"

Slumped in his seat, discouragement and frustration were written all over him. This was not like Ry.

"Is it money?" She could understand that.

"I've got the money, Doc," he said wearily. "I had a rich grandma who left a trust fund that would pay for med school several times over."

Doc felt shocked to her boots. Ry lived as conservatively as she did and worked overtime just as much. He had money and didn't use it? The guy was an idiot.

"Yesterday I told my dad and my sister that I was thinking about med school. This morning, I get home and there are two medical school applications in my mailbox. One for here in New York, the other in L.A. I don't know how they could have pulled that off, and it was probably Dad, not my sister, but it's just another example of how the family wants to run my life."

If she had support like that, to say nothing of the money and the college degree, she'd be the happiest person in the world. He sounded as if he'd been shackled, chained and spit up on. Maybe he ought to be, the ingrate.

Gall rising in her throat, she steered the bus to the first available curb, put the transmission in Park and turned to face her idiot partner.

"Ry, I still live with my parents so I can save every dime. I'm working on my degree, but only part-time. I have no friends, no freedom, no fun. And, if I can maintain this grueling lifestyle long enough to get my bachelor's degree, I plan to apply to med school myself. Of course I'll have to pray for admission because my grades aren't so hot, and if accepted, I'll have to mortgage my future with loans."

Ry couldn't believe it. This was Doc's secret life? Bless her heart, who wouldn't be cranky with that schedule?

"On the other hand, you already have a college degree. You have a *trust fund!* You have a family who sends you applications, probably to support and encourage you, not run your life. You say you want to do more, but you're here, working a job that no longer gives you satisfaction. How am I doing? Have I left anything out?"

He looked out the window and muttered,

"I think that about covers it."

"No, one more thing. For the past several months, I've seen you read your Bible when we get a break. I'd like to ask you, on what page does it say it's okay to waste your time doing less than you can?"

He had to take issue with that. "Being a paramedic isn't a waste of time, Doc. I've loved it."

"Are you saying you love it now?"

No, he couldn't claim that.

"I'd give anything to have what you're throwing away!"

He'd had about enough of this. "That's a great idea, Doc. *You* use my trust fund."

She slammed her hand down on the steering wheel. "That is so stupid, I'm through talking to you."

That was convenient, because he was through listening.

She started the engine, pulled away from the curb and drove straight to the station house without speaking to him again. From the jut of Doc's jaw, he'd say it was a good thing their shift was over.

His flash of anger had already settled down, and guilt set in. Doc had merely told it like it was. Here she was killing herself to get what he already had, and he didn't appreciate his advantages and opportunities enough to use them. He gotten so used to going his own way in life that he'd forgotten he was a Christian whose life was not his own anymore. The Word had plenty to say about a person who wasted what he'd been given.

It wouldn't be a waste to support Doc with a full scholarship from an anonymous donor. He could set that in motion. And he probably ought to take a good look at those application forms for himself.

With only two weeks into the new year, Meg felt she had the right to be rather pleased with herself. Not only had she identified two candidates for Mr. Right, she had already dated them both. The butterfly troop hadn't bothered to show up for either guy, but she'd accepted second dates from both of them. That was the deal, after all — to give love a chance to grow. Life was full of opportunities to trust God.

Or that's what she told herself when she wanted to give up on her New Year's resolution. It was depressing, facing the future without the butterfly troop. How could they ignore great guys like Kevin and Jonathan, yet perform fancy loops at the mere sound of Ry's voice? The last time the troop had made an appearance was when Ry called to see if she'd gotten home safely from the airport.

She ought to call Ry right now, strictly as a scientific experiment, just to see if the troop was voice activated. Even if she only got his voice mail message, they might be happy.

She punched in his number and the troop spiraled wildly at the mere prospect of talking to their guy.

"Hey, Power Woman," Ry answered, sounding happy.

He knew it was her? That meant he'd added her number to his caller ID — such a little thing, but it pleased her so much. The troop liked it, too. They whirled about and made her heart race. "How's New York City?" she said, breathing as hard as if she'd worked out.

"Cold," he said. "How's L.A.?"

Too far from where you are. Lonely without you. "Perfect," she said, putting a smile in her voice so she wouldn't give away how lonesome she was without him. "I had the top down on the convertible today. How was your day?"

"Too cold for the top down, that's for sure. Today was my last day working with my partner, Doc. She quit just after I got back and worked out her two-week notice.

I'll miss her, but she's going to college full-time, and that's good."

"What's she working toward?"

"Doc wants to be a real doc."

"How do you feel about that?" She held her breath, knowing this was a sensitive area for him.

"A person ought to follow her dream, don't you think?"

"Sure, as long as it doesn't rob anyone else of theirs. Is Doc married? Does she have a family, close friends, special people in her life? If she does, she might as well tell them goodbye."

"It doesn't have to be that way, Meg."

Maybe not, but that's how it was when Beth went to med school. But she hadn't called Ry to hold a pity party.

"We taped four shows this week," she said, changing the subject, "and tonight I'm field producing a dream date."

"What do you do when you 'field produce'?"

"We go along on the couple's dream date, record parts of it and show it on a future telecast. Since I was promoted to casting the show, I don't do much of that anymore."

"Beth says the ratings for *Dream Date* have gone up since you've been in your new job."

That was nice of Beth to brag about her.

"Did you match anyone today?" he asked, teasing.

"I found a guy who's a perfect match with my List."

There was a pause, and then he said, "Good for you."

"And I've had second dates with two excellent Mr. Right candidates." She tried to sound positive, which wasn't easy when she already regretted her vow to give love a chance to grow. It had taken real willpower to date those guys.

"Which one of them seems like a better prospect?"

It was just like the old days, with her talking about boys that she didn't care about just so she could talk to Ry. "They're about even."

"Tell me about them. Maybe I'll notice something you didn't catch."

He was serious. That made her smile. He might be an excellent judge of character, but she was the one who actually got paid for sizing people up.

"They both go to my church," she offered.

"That's good. And they both eat healthy and work out."

She laughed. He was quoting from The

List. "They look as if they do. Especially Kevin Fletcher. The man is really built."

"Hmm, how's his ego? Sometimes body-builders enjoy the look of themselves in the mirror a little too much."

That was funny coming from a guy who should know. "I'm sure I like his looks better than he does."

"I thought 'good looks' wasn't on the list."

"It isn't, but I'm not going to disqualify Kevin for being great-looking even if he isn't a very good dresser."

Ry laughed as she hoped he would do.

"Kevin's taste in clothes is awful, but a woman in his life could change that, don't you think?"

"It's been known to happen," he said dryly.

"Did I mention Kevin is our children's pastor? He's wonderful with the little kids. Everybody loves him. The only thing, Ry . . . He's a few years younger than I am, and he still lives with his mother. Do you think that's a problem?"

"Only if his mom is still laying out his clothes. Don't worry about the age thing. You're young at heart. Kevin sounds like he's the one. Congratulations, babe."

"But you haven't even heard about Jonathan Tremayne."

"I don't think I have to. Kevin seems perfect."

"But my date with Jonathan was so romantic. He really knows how to treat a woman."

She heard a choking sound. "Ry?"

"Just a minute," he said in a strangled whisper, followed by big clearing-the-throat sounds.

"Ry, are you okay?"

"Fine," he responded, his voice extra raspy, extra deep. "A sip of coffee went down wrong. You were saying . . . ?"

"Jonathan Tremayne is a business associate of Pete's. He just started attending our church."

"Is he at least as old as you?"

He made it sound as if she were middle-aged. "I thought age didn't matter."

"You're right. It doesn't. So what has Jonathan got to offer other than romance?"

"It's not on The List, and it isn't important to me, but Pete says he's very successful. Pete also says that ever since Jonathan found the Lord, he's been wife shopping."

" 'Wife shopping'?" Ry laughed until she thought she was going to have to hang up on him. "That's real romantic."

"That's not different than what I'm

doing. Maybe he's got a list of his own."

"You're right," he said, settling down. "How's Jonathan's taste in clothes?"

"Great. He doesn't need any help. But I might. He looks better than me."

"Babe, I guarantee he does not look better than you, and he's not going to care what you're wearing. You're the catch, Meg. Not him."

That was a sweet thing for him to say. "You're prejudiced," she said, wishing he were here in the room.

"Well, I do have a thing for dark-haired, blue-eyed Irish women."

The butterfly troop flitted as if their lives depended on motion. His buttery baritone made her think of moonlight, roses and a trip to New York in the dead of winter. She had some unused vacation days. Would he want to see her?

Moonlight, roses and candlelight on a terrace overlooking the Pacific — that was Meg's workplace tonight. From her position behind a potted palm, she watched the *Dream Date* couple at a cozy table for two.

The pretty blonde was a kindergarten teacher named Tami, and the quiet, dark-haired guy was a mechanic named Stan. In their formal clothes, fresh from their makeover sessions, Tami and Stan could have passed for movie stars. If ever there was a dream date, this was it.

The splash of ocean tide against the rocks below vied with piano music being played nearby. White linen, sparkling silver, tinkling crystal and a couple falling in love — that's what millions of viewers would see, and they would love it.

Meg put another notch in her matchmaker belt. At work they said it was uncanny, the way she scheduled the right combinations, but she thought anyone might fall in love in a setting like this.

She ought to test the theory on herself. Kevin couldn't afford this place unless she could get them a discounted rate, but Jonathan could. She could see the two of them there, Jonathan in a tux and herself in white with a long scarf that would float in the breeze. She would wear her hair long, pulled up on one side and fastened with a gardenia.

Actually, with her dark hair, Ry would be a better partner since Jonathan's coloring was so much like her own. Ry in a tux, his eyes intently on hers, while a smile deepened those dimples. Her heart beat madly, knowing —

"Meg." The irritated growl of Brad, her

camera operator, came through her headset.

She covered her mouth and whispered into the mike of her headset, "Brad, are you getting this?"

"I'm getting it, but, Meg, c'mon! This is *bor-ing!* Have 'em do something. We can't use any more of this."

Brad and his attitude. If he wasn't so good at his job, he'd be looking for work. But he was right. They'd shot Tami and Stan getting in and out of the limo; they had them watching the ocean at sunset, and they had Stan stealing a kiss. But they needed something that would make this segment pop, something that would make the studio audience laugh, moan, groan, sigh — anything, as long as it was big emotion. That was what made good TV.

Usually creativity on a shoot was Meg's strength, but tonight she had been so caught up in her own fantasy that she drew a blank. What could she have them do? It looked like she'd have to resort to the old finger-feeding ploy.

Strolling over to the couple, she put a big smile on her face. Compliment them first. Even the most confident *Dream Date* contestants were nervous in front of the camera.

"You both look fabulous," she said encouragingly.

160

Tami, who'd confided that she hoped this shot would lead to an acting career, fluffed her hair and looked directly at Brad's camera — which she'd been told not to do.

"Really?" Her wispy light voice sounded familiar.

"Hello, Marilyn Monroe," Brad said in the headset.

Meg ignored Brad and noticed that Stan was wearing clear nail polish tonight. His cuticles were in better shape than hers. "Having a good time, Stan?"

"Oh, baby," he said, his lip curled like an Elvis Presley wannabe.

In her headset, Brad burst out laughing. "Ladies and gentlemen, The King has entered the building."

"How are your appetizers?" she asked, ignoring Brad.

"I don't know," Tami said, looking down at her appetizer as if she hadn't noticed it was there. "I've been listening. . . . Oh, Stan, do you mind if I tell Meg what you just told me?"

With a suave wave of the fork in his hand, Stan granted permission.

"Stan says he knew I was the one for him the first moment he saw me on the show. Can you believe that?"

Meg smiled. She had pegged them to win

when she made out the schedule. "Before we wrap up the shoot and leave the two of you alone, we just need one more thing, something a little special, perhaps something a little more intimate."

"Oh, baby," Stan intoned again with a silly half grin.

"I was thinking you might feed each other bites of your appetizers."

"Feed me first, Stan," Tami said.

Meg murmured into her headset, "Brad, stand by for a close-up of Tami. We're finger-feeding."

"Gotcha." He moved to one side for a better view.

Stan took one of his oysters on the half shell, squeezed lemon juice on it, leaned toward Tami and slid the oyster into her mouth. She closed her eyes and acted as if it were the most delicious thing ever.

Meg turned away, the better to control her gag reflex. She wouldn't eat raw oysters for any man. Maybe Tami was a good actress. She spoke softly into her mike. "Did you get that, Brad?"

"Oh, baby," he said, mocking Stan.

Tami picked up a piece of her fancy Thai appetizer that looked like a glorified egg roll to Meg, although it did come with an orchid on her plate. She hand-fed it to Stan.

He chewed, swallowed and took Tami's hand, kissing the fingertips.

Meg could barely look, it was so silly.

"Oh, no!" Stan abruptly stood, frantically patting his tux pockets. "I don't have it with me."

"What, Stan? What's the matter?" Meg said, moving into the shot. It wouldn't matter. They couldn't use this.

"My shot. I don't have my shot. Call 911." He slumped in his chair.

"What's the matter?"

"Call it in. Now!"

Meg whipped out her cell phone and placed the call. She could see for herself that the man was in distress. Right before her eyes, Stan's face swelled, contorting horribly. His throat must be closing because his breathing was terribly labored.

Tami wrung her hands. "Do something, somebody!"

Guests from the nearby tables looked alarmed. Some rose from their seats to get a better look.

"Is there a doctor here?" Meg called out.

No one responded, but the maitre d' hurried to their table. "Should I call 911?"

"I already have. Have someone watch for the ambulance," Meg said, kneeling beside Stan. "Have you had this before, Stan? Do you know what's wrong?"

He nodded. "Peanuts," he said, gasping.

She checked their food. "You didn't have any peanuts."

The maitre d' looked over their food. "The lady's appetizer is prepared with peanut oil. Did you have some of that, sir?"

Stan nodded, fear in his eyes.

Tami sobbed. "This is all my fault."

Meg's heart sank. She was the one who'd suggested this. She was the one to blame.

Weakly, Stan tugged at his black bow tie.

"Let me do that," she said, brushing his fingers aside to unsnap the tie and undo his top shirt buttons.

"Is he going to die?" Tami cried. "Don't die, Stan."

"Meg!" Brad's stage whisper got Meg's attention. He waved her out of the shot.

He was taping this disaster? "The shoot's over, Brad," she muttered into her headset. At the sound of an arriving ambulance, she said, "Hang on, Stan. The paramedics will be here any second."

Almost unconscious, Stan fell from his chair, and the maitre d' eased him to the floor. Meg held his head, and the waiter frantically fanned Stan with a starched linen towel as if that would help.

Meg had never been happier to see

anyone than the pair of paramedics. In perfect unity, they calmed Stan, gave him medicine and worked swiftly and competently, their professionalism something to admire.

This is what Ry did, helping people, saving them. Meg couldn't wait to tell Ry how much she valued the work that he did. Maybe she should tell him in person. The troop fluttered madly in her stomach just thinking about it. To see that deep-dimpled smile, she might be able to fly to New York on the power of butterfly wings alone.

Chapter Eight

Whump . . . whump . . . whump.

Meg lay in her bed, her eyes on the ceiling, following the sound of the new guy upstairs bouncing a basketball from the bedroom, through the living room, to the tiny kitchen and back again. Since all of the apartments at Los Palmas had identical floor plans, she knew exactly where he was. And she knew exactly where she'd like him to be.

"Take it outside," she yelled. There was a very nice hoop and a fenced-in court where New Guy could play. He'd have no trouble finding a pickup game.

Whump . . . whump.

She should call the bikini twins, and have them entertain him. Meg didn't know what the twins did for a living but they had more bikinis than Meg had bridesmaid dresses, and nothing happened at Los Palmas that they didn't know about. They would knock on a person's door, offer freshly baked coffee cake and leave fully informed.

Just yesterday, the twins had showed up when she was packing her carry-on bag for her overnight trip to Honolulu. Before she knew it, she was telling them about Stan's problem, and they were assuring her she wasn't to blame.

The honchos at *Dream Date* apparently thought differently. Before Stan was released from the hospital, they'd offered him a second date with Tami and sweetened the deal by sending them to Hawaii in exchange for Stan signing a liability waver.

Her boss had ordered her to make sure all went well, and it had if she didn't count having Brad by her side the whole time. Everyone seemed to be happy except her, and that was her own fault.

Whump . . . whump . . . whump.

If she hadn't called Ry or left those two messages on his voice mail, she wouldn't have been so disappointed when he didn't call. Just because the butterfly troop thought that Ry was her guy, it didn't mean that he saw her as more than a grown-up version of his Li'l Sis. He cared for her, she was sure of that, but she'd jumped the boundaries of their friendship, and she wouldn't do it again.

Whump . . . whump.

"I can't believe this guy," she moaned, covering her head with her pillow. "Please, give it up."

The twins said that New Guy had been so charming they'd learned nothing about him. All they could report was that he had great muscles, a great smile and a great big TV and an SUV. Meg wished he'd take that ball for a ride in his SUV.

Barb, the prior tenant, had been such a nice, quiet girl and just perfect for Tony, the good-hearted camera operator at work. Too bad she'd moved in with him when they got married.

Whump . . . whump . . . whump.

Her bridesmaid dress for Barb and Tony's wedding had been yellow, her first yellow bridesmaid dress.

Whump . . . whump.

That was one of the problems, getting couples together. When they got married, they thought they had to express their grati-tude by having her in their wedding party.

Whump . . . whump . . . whump.

She couldn't seem to get it across that they didn't need to honor her that way. It was expensive, being a bridesmaid, and de-moralizing, never being the bride.

Whump! Whump! Whump!

He was louder than ever. "Hey, New Guy!" she yelled, for her benefit if not his. "There's a woman trying to sleep down here! Did your mother teach you nothing?"

Whump! Whump! Whump!

He might be a great-looking guy, but that didn't make him special, not in her book and not at Los Palmas. Hunks were everywhere — at the pool, the hot tub, the tennis courts, the parking lot. She'd recruited quite a few for the show.

Whump! Whump! Whump!

Good-looking men were way overrated. Her Mr. Right would have more brain than brawn. She wanted a guy who didn't have to watch the *Three Stooges* for a laugh and who could name the books of the Bible faster than he could recite the Lakers' starting roster.

Whump! Whump! Whump!

Meg threw the covers aside and came out of the bed with vengeance in mind. Enough was enough. Rounding the bed, she stubbed her toe on the corner of the bed frame.

Wow, did that hurt! Hopping around on one foot, holding her wounded toe, her shin connected with the sharp edge of the dresser. More pain! Tears in her eyes, she gritted her teeth.

Whump! Whump! Whump!

That was it. More than she could handle.

She hobbled to the utility closet, grabbed the broom and jabbed at the ceiling. Boomp! Boomp! Boomp!

"Don't make me come up there!" she yelled.

Whump! Whump!

She jabbed again, repeating his double. Boomp! Boomp!

A second of silence, and then four rapid whumps even louder than before.

"What's the matter? You need it in writing?" Jabbing hard, she repeated his sequence of four.

Silence again, then a single, hard . . . Whump!

"You heard me right." She answered with a single, heartfelt jab.

A minute passed, then two. Blissful silence. Meg smiled. Victory was sweet. It would be sweeter still if that last jab hadn't poked a hole in her ceiling.

And then it started, unending bounces of the basketball from hell. From bedroom to kitchen and back again until she wanted to scream.

She shimmied into a pair of jeans, left her nightshirt on and hobbled barefoot upstairs, so intent on confronting her tormentor that she barely felt the pain in her shin and her toe. Let New Guy see that a crazy woman lived in the apartment below. Let him worry about the heinous things that could happen if he weren't a good neighbor.

How long would he have to keep bouncing this basketball? Nobody could sleep through racket like this. Maybe she wasn't home, although the coffee cake twins assured him she was.

Those girls made really good coffee cake. He'd gone through half a cake, eating as he bounced the ball through his new apartment. A trail of crumbs attested to that.

The ferocious pounding on his door made him laugh out loud. Finally!

He peered through the peephole. Wooey! That was one mad lady outside. He grabbed a rose from the bouquet on the kitchen table, hid it behind his back and opened the door.

"I wondered how long it would take to get you up here," he said, laughing at the expression in Meg's big blue eyes.

"You!" She sagged against the door in complete shock.

"Did I wake you?" Ry didn't really have to ask. Her sleep-tousled hair, wrinkled nightshirt and jeans said it all.

She nodded, apparently speechless.

Some girls weren't very pretty until they

were all made up, but he loved the way Meg looked, all sleepy-eyed and natural. "I'm sorry I woke you, Meg. Maybe this flower will say it better than I can."

She took the flower, but held it, trance-like, as if she were stunned. He'd dreamed of her falling into his arms, but apparently she needed a moment to shift gears. That was understandable. The last time they'd talked, he'd ignored her hint that she would like to come to see him.

He'd hated doing that to her, though, on another level, it was wonderful to think Meg was missing him like he was missing her. If he hadn't already turned in his notice and made plans to come here, he'd have paid her way to New York and given her a welcome she'd never forget. Some day he would take her back and show her the city he'd loved.

"So what were you hitting the ceiling with?" he asked conversationally, praying that he hadn't judged this wrong.

"What are you doing here?" she murmured, ignoring his question and staring at him as if he weren't real.

"I live here. I moved in yesterday."

She looked at his unpacked boxes. "You live here?"

It probably was a lot to take in. "I sure do."

She had that shocked, but happy look that a person has when friends yell, "Surprise!" It was all he'd hoped for.

The three weeks it had taken him to close down his life in New York had seemed like three years, but they were proof to him that Meg was the woman for him. He'd never missed anything or anybody the way he'd missed her. Only the anticipation of this moment kept him going, and this was only the beginning. He planned to make her happy the rest of their lives.

"We're going to have fun being neighbors, aren't we, Meg?" He hoped they wouldn't be neighbors for long. They could go straight to a house with a white picket fence as far as he was concerned.

"I'm speechless," she said unnecessarily. He could see that for himself.

"How about a 'welcome to the neighborhood' hug?" He opened his arms, inviting her to step inside the apartment, and much more, inside his life.

Without hesitation, she wrapped her arms around his waist, laid her head on his shoulder and squeezed him so tightly, he could have shouted for joy. He hadn't been wrong. She wanted him here.

"I was worried that you might not be glad to see me," he murmured, loving the soft feel of her hair against his face.

"I thought you were mad at me," she said, her voice muffled against his chest.

"What for? When have I ever been mad at you?"

"But you didn't answer my calls."

"I didn't want to risk spoiling the surprise."

"Since when do I like surprises?" She glanced up at him with a frown.

"I know you don't like bad ones, but don't you like good surprises?"

"Not much. I like to know what's going on."

He probably ought to remember that.

"But I'm so happy to see you that there won't be much retribution this time."

Laughing inside, he tried to appear penitent. *"Much?"* he repeated. "Does there have to be any if I promise it won't happen again?"

She cocked her head to one side, considering.

He wasn't worried. He knew Meg, and she was his, whether she knew it right now or not.

"Just tell me how you managed to move in here," she said, stepping completely out of his arms and edging past him to make herself at home on his new black leather sofa.

He'd imagined the two of them on that sofa when he told Beth to order it. He sank down beside her and dropped his arm around her shoulders, old-pal style. He couldn't resist touching her. "Beth told me about the apartment," he said. "She set everything up."

Meg could hardly believe it. Beth was her lifelong best friend. They'd never had secrets from each other, yet she'd done all this? "When did all this happen?" she asked.

"Right after I got back to New York. I called and asked Beth to find me a place."

"You knew then?" Was it possible for butterflies to execute rollover flips?

He nodded. "I couldn't believe how much I missed . . . palm trees."

"Palm trees," she repeated, a bubble of excitement starting in her heart.

"Yes. Palm trees. Can't get enough of 'em."

"Is that right?" She laughed softly, delighting in the happiness in Ry's gray-green eyes. "Then, you must be in the right place. We have lots of palm trees at Los Palmas."

"I know! That's why I wanted to live here." His big, wide smile was contagious.

She had to laugh. "Lucky for you there was a vacancy."

"That's what Beth said, but I told her it

was God's timing, not luck. And she said she was starting to believe that herself. Isn't that great?"

Meg nodded. It would be if Beth weren't laughing at them both. She'd gone to a lot of trouble to prove that Meg and Ry were a "match made in heaven."

"What reason did you give Beth for moving back here?" she asked, scooting out from under his arm to retrieve the basketball he'd left by the door.

"I told her that I wanted a chance to be a better son."

A better son? Ry wasn't the one in that family who needed improved behavior. Sure, he'd been a rebel, but he couldn't agree to be his grandfather's clone just to please his mother. And nothing less would satisfy her.

She passed Ry the ball, and he smiled, catching it and tossing it back. It took a couple of passes back and forth and the steady influence of Ry's heart-lifting smile for Meg to feel her anger at his family ebb away.

He had asked if they would have fun, being neighbors. She would guarantee that. The love she felt for Ry was even bigger now than when they'd been kids. It was a crushing sensation, an overwhelming feeling she couldn't begin to put into words, but his happiness was a top priority. No matter how his family treated him, he could count on her.

Ry wanted her to be his fun neighbor. She could play that part. "I think we ought to talk about good neighbor etiquette," she said to get the fun going.

"What do you have in mind?"

"To begin with, people don't bounce basketballs in their apartments."

Ry had to laugh. That was Meg, giving him a lecture laced with sass.

"I think you need to make a significant gesture for waking me up," she said sternly.

"Name it," he said, smiling inside. Anything she wanted was hers.

"For starters, I think I'll take this basketball."

Well, maybe not. "What if I just promise to keep it in the closet until I take it outdoors?"

"What if you promise to let me play, too?"

The little shrimp thought she could play with him? "You'll need some help." He used to take on Meg and Beth . . . and let them almost win.

"I can get the help."

"Who from? The coffee cake twins?"

She reached over and brushed crumbs

from his T-shirt. "They said they'd met you."

"They ruined my surprise?"

"No, they didn't remember your name." She seemed to enjoy that. "But they described you perfectly."

"Tall, buff and handsome?"

"No, just tall . . . with a big TV."

He chuckled softly. The woman would not give him a break, and he loved it. "Hey, I've thought of a way I can apologize for disturbing your beauty sleep."

"It better be good."

"It is." She ought to love this. "I'm going to let you decorate my new apartment."

She lifted her brow skeptically and scanned the cardboard boxes, the big-screen TV and black leather sofa. "How could I improve on this? You have the minimalist look down to perfection."

"You don't think it needs a woman's touch?"

"Not this woman."

He'd thought she would jump at the chance to show what she could do. Every other apartment he'd lived in, some woman had stepped in to make his place feel like home.

"I've got it!" she said. Her face lit up like he'd hoped it would when he opened the door. "It's the perfect significant gesture, Ry."

"Drop it on me."

"You can be a *Dream Date* contestant! I'll get you scheduled for the show right away."

Not that again. Talk about a one-track mind.

"I've got an application downstairs." She headed for the door. "I'll get it, and we'll fill it out."

They could fill out the form or talk about the weather. It didn't matter as long as they were spending time together. How soon could he make his move and kiss her the way he should have done the last time he was here? Their first real kiss was way overdue. The New Year's Eve kisses were great, but they didn't count. He hadn't known then that she was meant to be his.

"You're going to make a fabulous contestant, Ry!"

She seemed so happy that he almost felt bad, knowing he would never go on her show. He hadn't moved three thousand miles to be with anyone but her. "Hurry back," he said as she was almost out the door. "I could use some help unpacking these boxes."

She looked back inside and lifted one brow, eyeing the mess. "On second thought, why don't you come down to my place? I'll make us breakfast."

Now *that* was more like it. "Okay, but I don't want you to go to any trouble."

"No trouble at all. Why don't you come down in a half an hour or so?"

He checked his watch. A half an hour. That meant she was going to do breakfast up right. Eggs, hashed browns, biscuits and sausage gravy, or his favorite — bacon and cinnamon French toast. He loved a good breakfast. "I'll be there. Can I bring anything?"

She glanced at his kitchen table and the huge vase of roses topping it. "Maybe you'd want to share a few more of those roses. You seem to have plenty."

"They're yours." For cooking such a good breakfast, she could have them all. Five dozen pink roses would look better in her apartment than in his.

Meg practically flew down the stairs to her apartment. Why had she given herself only thirty minutes? She could use that much time on the phone to tell Beth what a sneaky, conniving person she was.

Sure, this setup was Beth's way of having tons of fun, but it really wasn't right for Beth to mock Meg's belief in God. Besides, her prayer had been that the Lord would drop Mr. Right on her doorstep, not Mr. Temptation. The butterfly troop didn't seem to know the difference, but Meg definitely did. She'd been here before and knew this tingly sensation for what it was.

She'd been about thirteen when she first felt this way, and Ry had been fifteen with total bad-boy appeal. She'd loved it that he hadn't cared if he got into trouble, that he hadn't cared what people thought. This popular boy had listened to her and teased her so much that she'd wondered if he didn't see her as more than his Li'l Sis.

Now, it seemed that she would play the grown-up version of Li'l Sis, complete with the tingly crush. The thought was as exhilarating as it was daunting. Could she do that without losing her head over Ry?

It shouldn't matter what she wore around him, but she could do better than ratty hair and a wrinkled nightshirt.

After a quick shower, a little makeup, jeans and her soft blue sweater, she was almost ready. And her hair? Up on one side with a silver clip or smoothed back from her face and tied with a blue scarf?

"Meg?" Ry knocked on the door.

She left her hair plain and hurried to the door.

Pink roses filled the opening. "Where would you like these?" he said with a happy smile.

"How about the coffee table, once I get rid of . . . well, everything." It was the biggest bouquet she'd ever seen. "The roses are fabulous. Is it your birthday or something?"

"Or something." His tone would have discouraged most people, but she loved a good mystery. Who would send Ry flowers like these?

"Would you like some coffee?" she said, watching how carefully he placed the roses on her table.

"I never turn down cof—" He stared at her with the look of a man who liked what he saw.

The butterfly troop flew so happily that she touched her stomach, willing them to settle down.

"Gorgeous," she thought she heard him murmur.

"I beg your pardon." She had to hear that again. It shouldn't matter that Ry thought she looked pretty, but it did. It definitely did.

"Your apartment . . . it's gorgeous." He glanced about the room, his eyes lingering on her mother's artwork.

Well, that was a letdown. What was the matter with her? Was she thirteen again?

"I'm sorry the place is a mess," she said, regrouping the best she could while the butterfly troop danced for their guy.

He picked up her broom and eyed her ceiling. "Is this what you used to make that hole?"

"How could a few little jabs have done this much damage?" Chunks of plaster lay on the floor and a dusting of white powder covered a fairly large area.

"You're going to blame this on me, aren't you?"

Teasing, just like the old days — this she could handle. "It wouldn't have happened if you'd been a good neighbor."

"It's not my fault that you have a hair-trigger temper."

"Not anymore. I'm a calm, rational adult now."

He surveyed the mess. "I can see that. Should we call the super to fix this?"

She moved to the kitchen to pour coffee. "Los Palmas is a great place to live as long as you don't need repairs."

Ry started to collect the bigger pieces of plaster. "Is your waste can under the sink like mine?"

She nodded and stepped aside for him to

get to it. "You don't have to do this."

"Well, I wouldn't do it if I thought I had to. Where's your vacuum cleaner? In the utility closet?"

It was a little disconcerting to have him so familiar with her apartment. "Let it go. I'll clean up later."

"You cook," he said. "I'll clean."

From the corner of her eye, she watched him move, quickly making things right. He was an athlete, that was for sure, and a very smart guy. Not one motion was wasted. In seconds, he had his part of the job done.

"You know, you're really good at this," she said.

"You sound like my college roommate," he said, grinning. "His favorite spectator sport was watching me clean."

It could easily become her favorite, too. She might want to rethink that brain-over-brawn thing after watching those muscles at work.

He leaned on the counter while she cut up fruit and put it into the blender with milk, ice and protein powder. It made her nervous to have him watching her.

"This is nice," he said.

"I still can't believe you're here." With him standing this close, the butterfly troop believed it.

"I thought maybe you needed me," he said.

Her heart skipped a beat. "I needed you?"

"With your search for Mr. Right." He said that as if he truly planned to make that his agenda. "This is your year. You're going to find a guy who'll love you, who'll be a great husband and a great dad. I'm here for you, Meg."

The butterfly troop read way too much into that. If she left things up to them, they'd be booking a church and ordering invitations.

"You know," he said, staring at the ceiling, "I could fix that."

"You?" Her poor, tired brain couldn't catch up. She couldn't imagine Ry Brennan dealing with plaster.

"Sure. Don't you remember when I took that home maintenance course in high school instead of French III?"

"Your parents acted as if you'd joined a gang," she said, remembering it well.

"My proudest moment came when the powder room toilet wouldn't flush during one of their New Year's Eve parties. I fixed it while their colleagues watched."

"Yea, Ry!"

"I believe there was some grateful cheering."

"Led, no doubt, by your parents."

"Oh, sure, and they really loved it when Uncle Charlie slapped me on the back and said that Brennan Medical Clinic could use a good plumber. My dad gave him a black look and growled, 'Better a plumber than another urologist.' "

"Your uncle's specialty?"

He nodded. "For days, I talked about being a plumber."

"I'm surprised you didn't, just to spite them."

"I might have if Mitch hadn't died," he said quietly.

"That was a terrible time," she said, meeting his eyes, sharing the sadness of their friend's terrible car accident.

"The first responders really botched that job," Ry said bitterly, "first on the scene, and they compounded the problem by taking Mitch to the wrong hospital. When I didn't have a clue what I wanted to do, I thought about Mitch. If I became a paramedic, it might give his life meaning."

Her heart swelled with pride. "Any regrets?"

"Not really." His future was in the Lord's hands now. He'd done his part, applying to med school. Now he would see what the Lord wanted next.

Meg poured generous servings of her frothy fruity drink into tall glasses and topped them off with strawberries.

"These are almost too pretty to drink," he said, noticing that there didn't seem to be anything cooking.

"Would you like a piece of toast to go with that?"

"Yes, please." Nobody called him a picky eater, but he did prefer to eat his meals instead of drink them. From now on, he'd better do the cooking when they didn't eat out.

Sipping his drink, he admired the clean, sleek grays of her apartment, and how they were accented by the colors of her mother's art. "Are you sure you don't want to decorate my apartment? I love what you've done with yours."

Meg shook her head and smiled. "Talk to my mom. This is her work. She got a chance to mother me, and I got a chance to be an appreciative daughter."

"It's terrific, but I would have sworn you were more the hearts-and-flowers type."

Her pretty blue eyes laughed at him. "You're the one with the flowers. What's the story on those roses?"

"The card with the roses said 'Thank you.' "

" 'Thank you'?" Meg repeated skeptically. "For what?"

"Nothing special. But I lived in New York a long time. I made friends."

"Women friends," she said knowingly. "Tell me about her . . . or was it a group?"

He wasn't about to tell her that the card read, "One rose from each of the women you've left behind. New York's loss is L.A.'s gain." And it listed sixty women, starting with Nurses Tonya and Rachel. He hadn't recognized more than ten of the names, and he had a great memory. They'd gone to a lot of trouble and expense to make him smile.

"I'm waiting here," she said. "What's the story?"

He took another sip of his breakfast, not responding.

"You're not going to tell me, are you? Ry Brennan, you are amazing. You have this incredible talent for making women fall for you. You love 'em, leave 'em and they just keep loving you. How do you do it?"

"Meg, the roses were a joke."

"I don't know, Ry. Once a player, always a player."

"Hey! That's not fair." And this wasn't fun anymore.

"A leopard doesn't change his spots," she said firmly.

"This leopard is a one-woman guy." There. He'd said it. And if she didn't realize she was the one, she wasn't half as smart as she thought she was.

"If you're such a one-woman guy, let's get to work on that *Dream Date* application. I can't wait to see you walk away from the game show with the woman of your dreams by your side."

Only if it's you, Meg. Only if it's you.

Chapter Nine

The woman of his dreams had Ry tied up in knots. If it weren't for Meg, he'd be back in the heart of a New York City snowstorm, on the move, going from one call to another, doing some good. Instead he stood on a flower-lined driveway, hosing down an already-clean ambulance, just waiting for a call to come in. He would sure rather be treating a patient than shining up a bus.

Only, they didn't call the ambulance a "bus" out here. It was a "rig," and he worked a split-rig, meaning his new partner was an EMT, not a paramedic like himself. Hector Gonzales was a cocky guy with more energy than know-how, but at least he was a lot more fun than Doc.

Doc would have rolled her eyes at Hector's claim that he was God's gift to women, but Ry knew better than to take him seriously. Ry's only concern was how well they would work together on a serious trauma.

He'd gotten so used to working with Doc that he could tune out everything but the patient's needs, yet still hear her voice.

The adjustment to the new job had been more difficult than he'd expected. As an easygoing guy, few things really bothered him. Certainly he didn't mind the switch from a dark uniform to a light-blue shirt and navy cargo pants. He'd never worn boots to work before but he could see how they might come in handy on the variety of terrain out here.

In the suburban area they served, emergency personnel didn't have to wear bulletproof vests, or not often, and they wouldn't have to deal with elevators that didn't work or city traffic jams that left their patients waiting.

Instead of working out of an old, brick firehouse, he reported to an ordinary, white ranch-style house with an attached garage. Palm trees, not skyscrapers, lined the street, and there was such a laid-back feel that Ry should have felt right at home.

He didn't. Call him an adrenaline junkie, but he missed the noise, the crowds of humanity and the action. The private company he'd signed on with contracted with the fire department and did answer Code Threes, but much of their work was transport, not 911 calls.

On the other hand, the lack of action had given him plenty of time to think, and he'd come to two conclusions:

One was that Meg was meant to be his, and he would be so glad when she gave up this Mr. Right thing and realized he was meant for her. She'd filled a place in his heart he hadn't known was that empty.

It might be weak of him to admit it, but Meg got him. She understood him better than anybody. When he was with her, life was just . . . better. He felt centered, balanced, in the right place at the right time.

His second conclusion was he definitely wanted to be a doctor. In particular, he wanted to be an ER doc, and he wanted to work in a busy hospital where he could help lots of people. He wanted daily opportunities to use everything he knew, and he wanted more than fifteen minutes with patients before he dropped them off at an ER. He had loved being a paramedic, but he was ready for more now.

If he were a doctor, there would be the inevitable comparison to Trey that he would hate, and his mother would think she had won, but he could handle it. It was a great feeling to know he had a goal, a dream, a plan.

The scary part was that he might be too late in realizing it.

If he had applied to med school while he'd been in college, his grades and extra-curricular participation would have stood him in good stead with an admissions committee. But committees looked at things like why a student needed eight years to decide what he wanted. Who could blame them if they gave his slot to a younger applicant who would use that M.D. degree eight years longer than Ry ever could?

It would be so easy to worry about this, and it was so hard not to. If he didn't believe that God had a plan for his life, Ry knew he would choke on his daily prayer, "Your will be done." When a person wanted something as much as he wanted this, it was hard to see that God might want something different.

Asking Jesus to forgive his sins had been fairly easy, but surrendering his life, day by day, hour by hour . . . that was a whole different story.

The voice of their dispatcher broke into Ry's thoughts, a welcome interruption. It was a nursing home call, not his favorite, but a chance to be useful. Hector took the wheel and talked about girls the whole way there. Fortunately, it was a short ride.

The welcome they received at Willow Rest was one thing about the job that Ry loved most. People were so glad when help arrived. He never got tired of that.

The facility administrator led the way, reporting that an elderly gentlemen seemed to be in congestive heart failure. The nursing staff working over the man gave way for Hector and himself immediately.

Hector called the trauma center to report the CHF while Ry assessed the patient and noticed they were using a PEG tube to feed him through his stomach wall. If they had overfilled him, he would seem to be in CHF. It was easy to check. Quickly, Ry suctioned the man, and instantly, the patient was out of distress.

There was a small round of applause, but Ry ignored it and packed up his gear. It had probably looked more dramatic than it was.

Back in the rig, Hector said, "How did you know to do that, man?"

"It's no big thing to use training and experience when you have it. You'll get there, too."

Hector shook his head. "I don't think so. I don't think I'll stick around that long. I'd rather be a firefighter or a police officer. Better pay and all that."

Ry couldn't argue. People had to pay their bills. Most of the paramedics he'd known liked their jobs well enough, but they moved on for more money. Either that or they worked a lot of extra shifts. To keep from dipping into his trust fund, he'd done that himself.

"Why don't you become a nurse or a real doc?" Hector asked. "You're good, man, maybe the best I've seen."

"High praise for suctioning a PEG tube," Ry said in a lazy drawl to make light of the compliment.

"No, man, you're as good as the teachers I had. You know what you're doing."

"Let's hope so," Ry said, reaching for a bottle of water. He took a long drink and thought about telling Hector about those med school applications. If he got rejected, and he might, he'd didn't want to deal with pity — not from Hector, not from anyone.

"You don't talk about yourself much, do you?" Hector asked, giving Ry an assessing look.

Ry almost laughed. He wished Doc could hear that. "There are more interesting topics." Doc would second that.

"Not according to my little sister," Hector said with a sly grin. "Ever since she caught a glimpse of you when we drove by the neighborhood, she hasn't stopped talking about my new partner and his gorgeous dimples, his gorgeous smile . . ."

Ry groaned. Why couldn't Beth have been the only one to inherit his grandma's looks?

"His gorgeous, curly hair."

His low-maintenance hair. It had a life of its own. He missed Doc and her put-downs.

"My sister says you're 'eye candy,' partner."

"Tell your little sister to pick on guys her own age, and change the subject, Hector."

"Okay, we can talk about that little hottie nurse at the nursing home who was giving me the eye," Hector said.

Yes, they could . . . if there had been one. Ry did laugh at that. Doc wouldn't have seen the humor, but Ry sure did. Once upon a time, he might have said something equally silly, just to pass the time of day. But those days were over for him.

Meg was in big trouble. She sat at her desk with a pile of *Dream Date* questionnaires and couldn't seem to focus on a single one. This wouldn't do. She had shows to put together and applicants to contact for interviews, yet all she could think of was how much she wished she were with Ry.

That first week after his move to L.A. had been the best of her life. He'd had a whole week before his job started, and he spent it with her, waiting every night until she got home. No one was more fun than Ry, and they got along together terrifically. Besides their years of shared memories, they had their new faith in God to share, too.

She'd anticipated each new day with such joy, though the old tingles and flutters from junior high were a nuisance. The butterfly troop said she was falling in love, but they were new on the scene. What did they know?

Ry had a gift for making people feel special. He cared about them, and they took it for more than it was. If she let herself become another one of those women who misunderstood, she would have only herself to blame.

To keep that from happening, she had conscientiously introduced Ry to several women with Ms. Right potential — some at church, others at Los Palmas. It wasn't that he needed the introductions. He really was a chick magnet. But she would love to find him the perfect woman.

At least two had been excellent matches

in her professional opinion, and both made it clear they were interested. Ry made it just as clear that he was satisfied with her company alone. That, of course, was thrilling, but she had to face facts. This wouldn't last.

One day he would start dating for real. That was as certain as smoggy days in L.A. When that happened, she would be back in old-friend status, and the butterfly troop would resign.

She really should accept more first dates from Mr. Right prospects and more second dates, too. She'd spent way too much time with Ry, yet how could she not?

Beth was too busy for him. His coldhearted mother wouldn't even talk to him, and his dad . . . Well, his dad just made Meg mad. Dr. Brennan was all talk, giving Ry hope that they would have a relationship. He was no more of a dad now than he had ever been.

What a waste to have a son as wonderful as Ry and not cherish him. She wished the Brennans could see how sweet Ry was with Pete and Sunny's kids and how he never lost his temper. She'd begun to wonder what it would take to break through Ry's good nature.

For a new Christian, he seemed to connect with the Lord and show God's love better than anyone she'd seen. She wished she were as tolerant and easygoing as he was. Whether they were fixing up his apartment, driving out to Pete and Sunny's or just hanging out at their apartment complex, he just seemed so happy. That in itself was a wonderful testimony.

But now, she had to check the calendar to know when she might see him. Sometimes he worked one shift, then had one shift off. Other times he worked two, what he called "forty-eights," or he might work three or four shifts back to back with two or four shifts off.

And then there was the sleeping. If he hadn't gotten to sleep during his shift, he went right to bed when he got home. Naturally, she understood, but she still missed him even when she knew he was upstairs, asleep in his bed.

"That must be some applicant," Brad, her camera operator, said, coming up behind her. He slid into the seat beside her desk. "I caught you daydreaming, didn't I?"

"No." It was instinctive to deny it, especially to the most annoying person on the planet. "I was thinking."

He snorted. "Thinking about some guy."

She pointed to the application she'd been staring at. "Yeah, this guy looks like he'd be good on the show."

"Nice try! But that's not who you were thinking about. You were miles away from here. You know what I think?"

No, and she didn't care.

"Meg-gy's got a boy-friend," he sing-songed.

She rolled her eyes, and singsonged back, "Bradley makes up stories."

He laughed knowingly. "You can't fool me, Meg Maguire. You've got that 'down for the count' look. Who's the guy?"

"No guy, Brad," she said firmly, filing a couple of papers to look busy. Did she really have a "look"? That would be too humiliating.

"Oh, there's a guy, all right. I'd say that little Matchmaker Meg has finally met her match," he crooned with a grin.

Brad and his opinions. If he didn't have a question about work, he could leave. "How can I help you, Brad?"

"No, no. Let me help *you!* When you need dating advice, darlin', I'm your man. I've been around, you know?"

Poor Brad. A man who talked that much about his conquests probably had none. As irritating as he was, she ought to be kind. "It's nice to know I can count on you, Brad, but I'm still on my own, and I like it that way."

"Good for you, sweetness. Just keep telling yourself that. It won't hurt as much when that guy lets you down." He patted her hand sympathetically.

It was too much to bear, sympathy from Brad, the most pathetic guy she knew. "Look at the time," she said, pulling her purse from her desk drawer. "Got to go."

"I struck a nerve, didn't I?" he said knowingly.

Not at all, but Brad had plenty of nerve. "Have a good night," she said brightly, locking her file cabinet.

"Hey," he called after her, "seal the deal with this guy, Meg. You're not so young anymore."

She made it to her car without losing her cool, but only barely. Brad and his dating advice was enough to make a person scream. Seal the deal, indeed. As if she could. Holding on to Ry was like holding running water.

She pulled out of the parking lot and headed for home, praying as she drove.

Lord, more than anything, I want Your will. I want to show Your love and be a vessel You can flow through. You know how I feel about Ry and how he melts my heart. I want him to know what a good man he is and that he has nothing to prove. I want him to feel accepted just as he is.

But, Lord, protect me from caring about him too much. Don't let me get caught up in a longing that isn't meant to be.

The Lord never gave people too much for them to bear. When the time came that Ry didn't need her like he seemed to right now, she would be fine. Ry would never hurt her, not intentionally. He was the least hurtful person she knew.

The butterfly troop loved that about their guy — that, and his warm, caramel voice. And his eyes, not so much their color, but the way they looked at her with so much approval that she wondered how she had lived without it.

There were men who were more handsome, but Ry, with his high cheekbones and tapered jaw, had a lean and ready look that was totally appealing. And then there was his smile, that fabulous smile that just lit up his face.

If she ever got him on *Dream Date*, he would steal the show. The audience would love him, and the women contestants would, too. She could see it now, Ry taking it all in stride, letting none of it go to his head. That lack of ego was the mark of an adorable guy.

She could match Ry with someone wonderful. She really was very good at her job.

Why didn't she have him scheduled for *Dream Date* already? Usually, when she saw a perfect contestant, that person was as good as booked. She'd even gotten her brother to go on the show, and he'd been a total recluse at the time. Why was she letting Ry off the hook?

It wasn't as if they would stop being friends just because he found Ms. Right. They would still be great friends. They could even double-date. Ry in the front seat with Ms. Right. Her in the back seat with Mr. Right.

The butterfly troop didn't like that at all.

Over the top of his menu in the Mexican restaurant, Ry checked Meg out. He'd already decided on his order, but she always took more time. He didn't know why. He knew what she would order — some form of grilled chicken and salad — though she would change her order to match his after he ordered. It happened so often, he'd gotten in the habit of ordering things he knew she especially liked.

Tonight she wore her hair in yet another style. He didn't think he'd seen her wear it the same way twice in a row. This style left her slender neck bare and had a tousled effect that looked like he wouldn't mess it up if he followed his instincts and kissed his way up that slender neck to her pretty face and sweet mouth.

Tonight she wore pink gloss on her lips that matched her soft-pink sweater. It was a great color, and it was a great sweater. He liked all her clothes and the way she wore them, not so snug that a person who knew she was a Christian would doubt it, but just right. Her jeans and boots were black, and her black shoulder bag was big enough to park a small car in it. If it were as heavy as it looked, he ought to be the one carrying it.

The food server appeared and asked Meg for her order.

"I'll have the chicken Caesar salad."

Ry hid his smile. Now to see if his predictable girl would switch. "I'll have the chicken fajitas," he ordered.

Her eyes lit up. "That sounds good. I'd like to change and have that, too."

He loved it when she did that, as if they thought alike and were a couple. They did think alike so much of the time that he couldn't imagine them having a real fight.

The server left with their matching orders, and Meg folded her hands on the table, smiling at him so brightly that he braced himself for a Meggy Maneuver. He knew she was up to something.

"Tonight's the night," she said, those pretty blue eyes sparkling with confidence.

His heart bumped hard against his chest, reacting to her innocent comment the way he would have in his pre-Christian days. "What do you have in mind?" he asked, taking a sip of water while he marshaled those pre-Christian thoughts.

"Tonight we fill out your *Dream Date* application," she said as if she were doing him some great favor.

It felt more like a punch in the gut. Couldn't she see he didn't want to be with anyone but her?

"I haven't been fair to you, Ry."

Oh, no. That was the classic opening for a kiss-off. "Fair to me?" he echoed faintly, his heart in his throat.

"Yes. The way I've kept you to myself isn't right."

She was dumping him. What could he say to make it stop? "I don't think I've complained."

"I know, but I got to thinking about you today . . ."

That was good.

"And I thought that if I were a real friend, I would want to schedule you for *Dream Date*."

Okay, now he would complain.

"I want to see you happy with the woman of your dreams."

He already was happy with the woman of his dreams, or he would be if she would stop talking like this.

She dug in her big black purse and whipped out a pen and paper. Poised to write, she said, "Talk to me. If you could take someone special on the date of your dreams, where would you go? What would you do? The more details the better."

"Let me make it easy for you, Meg," he snapped, on the edge of losing his temper. "We'd be at a Mexican restaurant just like this one, and my date would put that pen and paper away and enjoy the chips and salsa."

Her eyes opened wide. "See! That's why you're going to be great on the show. That was a perfect 'bad boy' response. Our audiences love bad boys, and so few qualify."

Why was he so crazy about this woman? She might have trouble choosing what to order or how to wear her hair, but Meg Maguire was plenty strong-willed.

"You know, Meg, I'm not real sure what a 'bad boy' is," he said with a lazy drawl to cover his irritation.

"That's it!" she said, glowing. "It's the attitude. You said that like you didn't know and you didn't care. Women eat that up, Ry. They can't resist the challenge. They say to themselves, 'Can I make that bad boy care? Can I capture his heart and turn him around?' "

If that were true, Ry was no bad boy. Once, he may have been, but he no longer qualified. Meg had already captured his heart, and the Lord had turned him around.

"A true bad boy doesn't let anyone shove him around," she said brightly. "He does what he knows is right for himself. Sound familiar?"

Of course it did, but hadn't she seen how he'd changed? Did she really think he didn't care what she thought or that he only went after what was right for himself? A Christian didn't do that.

"If that's what you think, then you know I'm not going to do your show." He didn't care how hard that sounded.

"Did you follow the Knicks when you were in New York?"

"Of course," he said, glad of the change of subject. They could talk about the Knicks, eat their food and then he would take her home.

"One of the Knicks' players was on *Dream Date* last month. He was our first pro

207

basketball player, and you'll be our first paramedic."

In her dreams. He took another sip of water and looked toward the kitchen. Their food ought to be here by now.

"Another great perk is we provide every contestant with a network-quality recording of the show. It may not seem important now, but someday your children, even your grandchildren, will see the show and know, that once upon a time, their daddy — their granddaddy — was young and strong and good-looking and —"

"Meg," he interrupted before his temper boiled over. "In the interest of ending this so we can enjoy our dinner, may I make a suggestion? If you're that hard up for contestants, sign up my partner."

"Your partner?"

"Hector Gonzales isn't a paramedic, but he is an EMT. He's a genuine 'bad boy,' and he'd love to be on your show." There. That ought to end it.

She stared at him steadily as if she were considering the deal. "You really don't want a dream date?"

Not with anyone but her, and he wasn't so sure about that at the moment.

"I could find you someone perfect, Ry."

"I know you could," he said sincerely.

"Thanks for the offer, but no thanks. I don't need any help right now."

"Well, if you're sure. . . ."

She didn't seem all that disappointed. In fact, her smile was so wide, a person would think she'd just gotten her way. What was she up to?

Chapter Ten

Their food arrived, and, to his relief, Meg changed the subject and was her usual darling self. Sometimes he thought he couldn't stand this waiting for her to fall for him, and sometimes he wondered if she already had and only pretended to want his help in her search for Mr. Right. In truth, the search seemed to be only a token effort.

Could she be playing the same hide-and-seek game he was? As bad at words as he was, how could he find out?

A true bad boy would just ask.

"Are you going to give me the daily report on the Mr. Right search?" he asked, gathering his courage for what he really wanted to ask.

She played with her napkin, not meeting his eyes. "I'd think you would be sick of listening to me talk about my flawed love life."

Of course he was, but as long as her search was on, he wanted to be in on it.

Coaching from the sidelines, he could control the game. "But I'm believing with you, Meg. This is your year. Mr. Right *is* going to show up."

She loved that, he could tell. "You think so?"

"I do. For all we know, it could be me."

She choked on a sip of soda. "What?" she said in a strangled voice.

"Maybe *I'm* your guy. Did you ever think of that?"

She looked at him as if he couldn't be serious.

"Don't we always have fun together?" he said, touching her index finger with his, keeping it light, hoping she would see what he did.

"Of course we have fun together, Ry, but you have fun with lots of women."

"Lots of women?" Where did she come up with that? "Have you seen me with anyone but you?"

"No, but I happen to know that the bikini twins are taking a survey on which Los Palmas woman will be the first to date Ry Brennan."

Once, that wouldn't have surprised him, but it did now. "The bikini twins?" he repeated, wondering who would start such a stupid survey.

"Oh, you call them the coffee cake twins."

"Ah, Carol and Cheryl." Now he understood. They loved to joke around.

"See? That's what I mean. I can't even remember their names, but you can, and you've barely moved in."

"But I'm good with names, and Carol and Cheryl are nice people."

"They are, but that's not the point. My Mr. Right will think *I'm* a nice person. Just me, not one of the pack."

"I never knew you were the jealous type, Meg."

"I'm not." She threw her paper napkin at him.

He caught it, laughing. "You do sound kind of jealous, babe, but don't worry. I'll be true to you."

"That would be nice if you were a match for my list," she said sweetly, "but you're not."

"I'm a perfect match on that list," he protested, knowing he wasn't, not quite, but playing along.

"Let's just check that." She dug in her big black purse and produced a folded paper. "Number one — Mr. Right has to be Christian and go to church."

"That's me," he murmured, marking a tally in midair.

"That's every guy I've considered," she said, as if that ought to burst his bubble. "And few have made the cut."

He laughed, loving her sass. "What's two?"

"Two is that he has to be a best friend who'll want to spend time with me —"

"I'm here, babe." She had to see that for herself.

"But who was with me last night?"

She had him on that. "You're not keeping secrets, are you, Meg?"

"I don't keep secrets. You've known about every candidate, except the guy last night. That was Steve who just happens to be a fabulous chef. After he cooked dinner, he made himself at home on my sofa and we watched a praise-and-worship video together."

"It is a very comfortable sofa."

"I believe Steve said the same thing."

"Too bad Steve's not Mr. Right."

"And how do you know that?"

"You said he was a chef."

"What woman wouldn't want an in-house chef?" she asked as if he were absurd.

"You. You want a guy who'll want to spend time with you 'and have a job where he can.' "

She looked at the list. "That's a direct

quote. How do you do that?"

He shrugged. He'd always had a good memory. "A chef works a lot of hours, Meg, usually in the evening," he said. "Too bad for Steve, but he's out."

"Then you are, too. I can never remember when you're going to be working and when you're not."

Ry frowned, disgusted with himself for walking into that. He must really be tired. "Paramedics work eight-hour shifts in some places. We could move to one of them."

She had the nerve to laugh in his face.

He rubbed the back of his neck, trying to see the humor in it himself.

"Next is a good sense of humor. I don't see you laughing, Ry."

If a man couldn't laugh at himself, he wasn't much of a man. It wasn't that hard to come up with a smile, a genuine "I'm crazy about you" smile, and said, "I'm your guy, Meg."

She rolled her eyes. "Try that on someone who hasn't seen you use that look dozens of times."

Did she really think that badly of him?

"You'll like number four better," she said. "Remember that Beth insisted that we add 'not a doctor.' That ought to make you happy because you're not."

But he might be. "You wouldn't exclude a guy for that, would you? Maybe God wants your guy to be a doctor."

"I don't think so," she said firmly. "The Lord knows how lonely I was when I lost Beth to med school, and I've seen how your parents live. Why would I want that?"

Ry could see she was serious about this, and it just about broke his heart. She had been a Christian longer than he had, but he knew that God gave a person what was needed when it was needed, not necessarily before. And a person didn't slam a door on God's will just because it seemed too hard. They would have to work on this. "What's next?" he asked, his heart not really into this anymore.

" 'Five — he must have a dream and goals.' "

He had a dream, a very big dream, but this was not the time to share it.

"No comment?" she asked.

"I'm a match on the rest." He ticked off the remaining items, counting on his fingers. "Mr. Right must 'like and want children, like your friends, work out, eat healthy and save money.' Did I miss anything?" He knew he hadn't.

She scanned the list. "That's about it."

"Face it, babe. I'm your man."

"Care to prove that?" she asked sweetly. Too sweetly.

"Maybe. What do you have on your mind?"

She pulled the *Dream Date* application out of her purse.

"Not that again!"

"Relax. I'm not going to make you fill it out. We'll just use the categories to see how compatible we are."

That might work. He knew her pretty well.

"The first item is 'favorite food on a dream date.' I'm writing my answer down, then you can answer verbally."

She hid her paper from him, but he didn't care. He knew her answer, and he could match it.

She finished writing. "Okay, you first."

His favorite would be Greek specialties from Toula's in New York City, but he said, "I already told you. Mexican."

"You did say that," she admitted, frowning.

"Yes, I did. Are we a match?"

She nodded. "On that, we are. Next is 'favorite form of transportation.' "

She wrote her answer, and he considered the options. She loved her convertible, but for a dream date, he thought she'd like to go first-class.

She looked up at him expectantly.

"Limo. My girl deserves the best."

She frowned again, and he pulled her paper over to see what she'd written. Ha! Another match. This was working out very well.

"Lucky guess," she said. "Next is 'favorite music preference.' "

He knew they both had praise-and-worship CDs in their cars, but he'd heard her playing romantic ballads. Chick songs weren't his favorite, but he knew them well enough. He might forget to buy basics like milk and bread, but once he heard something, even a chick song, it stayed in his head. He answered with a couple of popular titles.

"I can't believe it," she said, staring at her paper. "You do not like those songs."

"Do, too. I think you're reading my mind," he said, pretending offense.

"I am not. But if you're a match on this next one, you might have Mr. Right potential."

Great! He always played well under pressure. "What's the category?"

" 'Describe your favorite dream date, start to finish.' "

He'd always hated essay questions. What would she say? Shopping . . . most women loved to shop. He'd start with that, then go with the Mexican food. Then they could take a drive down to Big Sur in that limo. Since he wouldn't have to concentrate on driving, it would be a perfect time to discuss important things . . . like the date of their wedding and how many children she wanted to have.

"What's your answer, Mr. Right?" she asked, grinning like she knew she'd won this round.

"No, you first this time."

"No way. You'll cheat and copy my answers."

"I promise not to." They weren't going to match on this, but he would remember what she said. She'd have her dream date with him, down to the last detail.

"My dream date would start in church," she said, "so we could worship together. Are you with me?"

He'd like to be. He nodded, loving her so.

"After church, we would take a boat to Catalina."

Oh, not so good. He got seasick before a boat left the wharf, and the pills to prevent it put him to sleep.

"My date and I would stroll past the little shops, but we wouldn't actually shop since I hate to shop."

He didn't know that. A woman who didn't like to shop? Talk about a gift. Meg was a jewel.

"We'd eat ice-cream cones, and later we'd have dinner at a beachfront restaurant."

He could do that, once he was over being seasick.

"We would listen to the waves, watch the stars and take the last boat back."

"Sounds like a great date," he said, imagining it all, right down to the image of himself at the rail, seasick once more.

"I would love that," she said with a dreamy expression.

"Better take a jacket," he said for want of anything better to say. "It gets chilly on the water, especially at night."

She laughed softly. "How funny. Ry, you sound just like somebody's mother."

He'd been called many things since he discovered girls. A charmer, a cheat, a two-timer and, one time, a skunk. But never somebody's mother.

Meg fastened her seat belt in Ry's SUV and wondered if she'd just given herself away. It wasn't easy to disguise how thrilled she'd been to have Ry suggest he might be Mr. Right. Of course, he was teasing, but it was pretty remarkable that he would even tease about that.

Could he see the two of them together? Could he be ready to settle down? It wasn't likely. She would have to be very careful. If he thought she took that seriously, he could disappear from her life like early-morning dew under the hot California sun.

She didn't want that — for either of their sakes. He needed her, both as a Christian friend and as an ally against his family. And she needed him because . . .

She couldn't name it, but she just did, for now at least. It would go away when she met somebody wonderful, someone who was clearly Mr. Right instead of Mr. Right Now.

Even though Ry had not liked it, she was glad that she'd pushed him to go on *Dream Date*. She'd given him a clear signal that he didn't have to hang around with her all the time just because they were old friends and new neighbors. It was up to him. He could go back to his old habit of dating a different woman every day anytime he wanted.

Liar. Big fat liar. The butterfly troop stomped on her stomach with heavy lead feet. And they were right. She loved being with Ry, and she would hate it when he moved on.

She glanced over at him behind the wheel

of his SUV, trying to gauge his mood. "Where are we going?" she asked as he exited the freeway.

"It's a surprise," he said in that drawl she loved, giving her a glimpse of his deep-dimpled smile.

She wasn't all that keen on surprises, but she did love that smile. What did it matter where they went as long as they were together?

He pulled into a new upscale shopping mall, one that she hadn't visited before, not that she shopped anywhere often. This one had the lush look of a desert oasis. He parked in front of a huge store for children and babies.

"I know you said you don't like to shop, but I was here the other day on a call," he said, putting the car keys in his jeans pocket. "It's a nice store. I thought we might get something for baby Meggy and Shay."

How sweet that he would think of her precious niece and nephew. Her heart swelled. Could her crush on him get any bigger? This was definitely worse than when they were kids.

"Shall we go in?"

Meg was ready to follow him anywhere.

They got out, and he took her hand. "I don't want to lose you," he said lightly. The way he held her hand, there wasn't a chance.

As long as they had known each other, Meg couldn't remember them holding hands like this. It felt as if they were a couple, two people who belonged to each other, spending an evening, happy together.

Such a mixture of contentment, elation and pride filled her mind that she couldn't stop smiling. Here she was, walking beside this gorgeous guy, a guy who wanted to buy presents for Shay and Meggy, a guy who loved the Lord, a guy who hinted that he might see a future for the two of them. He *could* be Mr. Right. In his khaki sweater and blue jeans, he looked rugged and all man. Her man, if only for now.

Inside the store, an awesome display of luxurious cribs stopped Meg in her tracks. "Wow," she murmured. "Isn't this great?"

When Ry didn't answer, she followed his gaze. Her most unfavorite couple, Trey and Isabel, were coming their way, laden with boxes and shopping bags, or at least Trey was. It looked as if it was all Isabel could do to carry her little purse and the baby inside her. The poor girl walked on puffy feet with that soon-to-deliver sideways sway.

"It looks as if we've come along at the right time," Ry said with a smile for Isabel.

He took part of Trey's load, but kept a free hand to steady Isabel.

Isabel looked at him gratefully, though she seemed too miserable to summon up a smile.

"I bet you'd like to get off your feet," Meg said, motioning toward a bench just inside the door. "It looks like you've bought out the store."

"Blame that on Izzie," Trey grumbled. "I don't know why she waited until the baby's due date to shop. After all the things Mom bought and all the baby shower gifts she received, I don't know why we had to shop at all."

"But I wanted you to help pick out things for the baby's room," Isabel said, her lip quivering. "And you never had time. All you ever do is work."

Meg could believe that. Poor Isabel.

"Don't put this on me," Trey said hatefully. "You're the decorator. You do your job, and I'll do mine."

Anger spiked through Meg's body. How could a man talk to the mother of his baby that way? Couldn't he see how miserable she was? Ry wanted to win Trey to the Lord, but Meg wanted something far different — something like slow, painful torture. Childbirth ought to be about right.

Isabel sank heavily onto the bench.

"Turn sideways, hon, and put your feet up," Ry said, putting the packages down to help her get settled.

"She's all right," Trey complained. "Come on, Izzie. I'm going home." He headed for the door.

Meg could not believe this guy. The least he could do was bring the car to the door for his wife.

"Trey, wait," Ry said. "Isabel, are you in labor?"

"I don't think so." A tear streaked down her cheek. "But I do feel terrible. I've had a backache all day."

"What do you think, Trey?" Ry said, deferring to his brother. "You're the doctor."

"I'm the neurologist," Trey said nastily. "Izzie can see her ob-gyn tomorrow."

"Trey . . ." Ry's calm voice had a warning tone. "You might want to take another look here."

"The day I take the advice of a paramedic is the day —"

Trey stopped midsentence, for he had indeed taken another look. Meg followed his startled stare.

Isabel's face crumpled, and she started to cry. Her water had broken.

Ry scooped her up in his arms. "It's going

to be fine, hon. You're all right. Where's your car, Trey?"

Trey looked shaken. "Uh, why don't we call an ambulance?"

"We can do that," Ry said calmly, "but while we're waiting, Isabel will be more comfortable in the privacy of your car."

"Let's, uh, wait for the ambulance. Why mess up my upholstery?"

Meg could not believe it. Was there nothing noble about Trey Brennan? No kindness? No sense of decency?

"I'll take her to my car," Ry said calmly. "Meg, call 911."

"I can call 911 myself," Trey whined. "I don't need your help."

"No, but your wife does," Meg said with disgust, brushing past him to hold the door open for Ry. She already had her cell phone out and the emergency number punched in.

"You handle the packages, Trey," Ry said. "We'll take care of Isabel."

"Put my wife down!" Trey's face contorted angrily.

Isabel clung to Ry and sobbed.

Meg wanted to cry herself, she felt so sorry for Isabel. This little family really needed to know the Lord, or none of them would know a happy life.

Chapter Eleven

Isabel's baby boy arrived just after dawn. Little J.T., as his parents were calling him — the birth certificate said James Thomas Brennan IV — weighed six pounds, six ounces and had dark hair like his mommy. Meg hoped that J.T. would grow up to be just like her. Isabel had shown a lot of character during the birth, and Meg decided she liked her after all.

Trey, however, was still as unlikeable as ever. His behavior during Isabel's labor had been a disgrace. The way he kept disappearing, it had been a good thing that Meg and Ry had been there for Isabel. Especially Ry.

Ry had been nothing short of wonderful. He might not be a doctor like the rest of the Brennans, but he was the Brennan Meg would want to have with her if she ever went through this ordeal.

But now Trey, the big phony, stood in the

nursery hallway with his parents, acting as if he'd been the one to go through labor. It made Meg sick.

Dr. Brennan got a good look at his grandson, then wandered off to see Isabel, which made Meg think better of him. But Deborah Brennan gushed over Trey, thanking him for this first grandchild, until Meg wanted to say, "Save that gratitude for Isabel. She's the one who deserves it!"

"Congratulations, Grandma," Ry said gently, touching his mother's shoulder.

Wasn't that just like Ry, trying again to build a bridge from their awful past to a happier future?

But his mother flinched at Ry's touch as if she'd been stung by a bee.

White-hot anger seared Meg's mind. How could Deborah do that? Was she mentally ill or just plain mean? Meg slid her arm around Ry's waist, praying that he would know he wasn't alone.

Ry drew her close, so close she could feel his body tremble. If she hadn't felt that, she might have given her prayer a chance to work. Instead, she went for a gibe that would put Deborah Brennan in her place.

"Ry, maybe your mother doesn't want to be called 'Grandma.' She doesn't really look like a 'Grandma' to me."

Deborah looked pleased. "Yes, I prefer 'Grandmother' or even 'Gran,' " she said imperially.

" 'Gran,' " Meg repeated, gleeful that Deborah had given her something to work with. "That's good, but how about 'Granny'? My grandmother loved to be called Granny Sue."

Meg almost laughed at the way the regal Deborah recoiled.

Meg leaned toward the nursery window and tapped lightly. "Hey, J.T., meet Granny Debbie."

Granny Debbie shot Meg a truly nasty look.

Meg didn't care, not at the moment.

Ry squeezed her shoulder and bit back a smile. She saw it. His mother did, too. Rage glittered in her eyes as she dismissed them with an offended sniff and marched down the hall. Trey trailed behind her like a whipped dog.

Ry gave Meg a rueful smile. "I don't think Granny Debbie's very happy with us."

She smiled up at him. "But we're used to that. Ry Brennan, you are the best, and don't forget it."

His mouth tilted, discounting the claim, but he leaned down and placed a kiss on her forehead. Longing to show Ry that he was a man worth loving, she rested her head on his chest and wrapped her arms around him. He cuddled her close as if she had made a good choice.

"Hey, you two." Beth came toward them, wearing scrubs and a stethoscope around her neck.

Last night Trey had directed the ambulance to Cedar Hills Memorial where the Brennans were known and where Beth worked, too. She'd popped in on them during the night.

"How's it going?" she asked.

"The baby's great," Ry replied with a tired but satisfied smile. "Isabel's fine, Mom's happy, Dad's proud, Trey's . . . Trey."

Beth chuckled at his restraint.

Meg didn't feel as charitable. "Actually, Trey's impossible. Beth, when we met them at that baby store last night, there was Isabel, about to give birth, and there was Trey, punching words in her face about how he did his job and she ought to do hers."

"He said that?" Beth asked, her lip curled.

"Apparently Isabel's 'job' is to live her life alone," Meg said, still angry about it. "Who would want to marry a doctor, no matter how rich he was?"

Beth glanced at Ry, and their eyes held

for a second as if they were thinking about the same thing, probably about the life their mother had lived, their grandmother and Isabel, too. Meg pitied them all.

"Who would want to marry a doctor?" Beth repeated. "As long as you asked, Meg, I'd say a woman who admires how much her man wants to make a difference and how serious he is about wanting to help people. Or maybe a woman who appreciates that her man is smart, incredibly dedicated —"

"And rich," Meg added. One of them ought to be realistic.

"That's not it, Meg," Ry said quietly.

Beth backed him up. "Most of the doctors I know didn't go into it for the money. By the time they get through school and start earning any money, they have to pay off school bills, then deal with the HMOs and liability insurance. It's not what people think."

It wasn't like Beth to lecture. What had happened to make her unload this way? On New Year's Eve, it was Beth herself who had ruled out doctors as Mr. Right candidates. Now she was changing her tune?

Maybe Beth felt insulted, being a doctor herself. "I'm sure you're right, Beth," Meg said apologetically, wishing she hadn't been so outspoken. As seldom as she saw Beth,

Meg didn't want to spend their time arguing.

"Check out the baby," Ry said, nodding toward the nursery window where tiny J.T. stretched in his sleep. "Look at those long fingers. I think he looks like a quarterback, don't you?"

Beth hooted. "Wouldn't it be perfect if he turned out to be everything you are and Trey isn't?"

"Don't wish that on the kid," Ry muttered. "He'll be looking for a new home."

Beth's eyes found Meg's. Ry had suffered more than they had known.

"The last time I saw Isabel, she was one grateful mommy," Beth claimed brightly, changing the mood. "She said you two were terrific."

"Ry was the one who was terrific," Meg said, looking up at him with the approval he deserved.

Beth smiled to herself, so glad that her brother had Meg to love him. And Ry was so in love with her that Beth felt positively teary. What she would give to be loved like that. Maybe there was a God. Her brother and her best friend did seem like a match made in heaven.

She couldn't resist teasing them. "It looks as if I was right," she said with a meaningful glance at Meg.

"About what?" Ry asked innocently.

But alarm flared in Meg's eyes. Beth almost laughed. It took so little to communicate with best friends who were on the same wavelength.

"Beth, why don't you go with me to the rest room?" Meg said, grabbing her arm.

"Why do women always need another woman to go to the rest room?" Ry said, shaking his head as they left.

Beth grinned back at him. "It's just part of the pairing-up instinct. Right, Meggy?"

"It's 'Meg'!" she snapped. "And you know that."

Beth did know, but if a scolding was coming, why not have a little fun first?

In the rest room, Meg squared off, her hands on her hips, ready for battle. "Okay, Beth, let's get this settled, once and for all. I know you're only kidding but —"

"Who said I was kidding?" Beth interrupted. She did so love to be right, and, boy, was she right this time.

"Well, you *have* to be kidding," Meg said emphatically.

"Nope, you and Ry are perfect together."

Meg rolled her eyes. "Beth, no matter what it looked like back there —"

"Like two people who are in love with each other."

232

"No! Like two people who were very tired and . . . rather emotional from such a big night."

"Meg, you don't have to justify anything to me. I'm thrilled that you and Ry are together."

"We are not together! It's only been a month since he came back into my life. It's little more than a week since he's moved back here. We are not together."

"Well, you looked pretty 'together' to me. A bug couldn't have crawled between you."

"That's disgusting."

"I thought it was kind of nice. And it's not too soon, not for you two. You've known each other forever. I've never seen a couple more in love."

Wild hope covered Meg's face, just for an instant, before worry took over. "You're not kidding? Did I really look like I was in love with Ry?"

"Oh, yeah," Beth said, bolstering Meg's confidence just like the old days when they were kids talking about boys.

"But Ry didn't see that, did he?" Meg said, her eyes worried. "Beth, if he thinks I've fallen for him, you know what will happen."

"Sure I do. He'll put a ring on your finger, and we'll be sisters for real."

Meg seemed to crumble. "That's not going to happen. If Ry thinks I care, he'll leave. Who knows if he'll ever come back?"

"Meg! How can you think that?"

"Because we know him. As soon as Ry realizes a woman is in love with him, he's gone and out of her life. We saw it over and over."

"That was when we were kids! Ry's a grown man who knows what he wants and, boy, does he want you."

"Beth Brennan, you will say anything to prove you're right."

"That's true, but my brother is crazy about you."

"You're doing that smirky smile thing, Beth."

"Well, it's hard not to smirk when I'm this right."

"Nobody likes a smirker."

Beth laughed out loud. Meg hated to lose an argument.

"For your information," Meg said, fire blazing in her blue eyes, "I have followed my New Year's resolution to the letter, and Ry has been a big help. I'm actively pursuing Mr. Right, and I've had a whole bunch of dates with eligible guys."

Poor, poor Meggy. Wasting her time. Ry wouldn't be about to let Meg fall for anyone but him. But Beth played the game and said, "Good for you. All first dates, Meg?"

"No! As it happens, I'm having my fourth date this week with a great guy who's our children's pastor."

Beth didn't like the sound of that. "Does Ry know?"

"Of course," Meg said with a smirky smile of her own. "He's known about them all, and he handpicked the children's pastor as the keeper of the bunch."

Beth couldn't hold back a loud guffaw. As a playmaker who'd quarterbacked high school and college football teams to championships, her brother would certainly know how to eliminate the competition. If Ry had endorsed the children's pastor, that guy was no keeper.

Ry began the drive home from work feeling more hopeful than he had since J.T. was born. Today, he'd seen Beth at the hospital, and she'd said it was only a matter of time before Meg admitted she was in love with him. He prayed his sister was right. It seemed like a long time that he'd been waiting for her to see that he was her Mr. Right. Maybe it was because he'd been waiting all his life for someone to love.

Valentine's Day was coming up in a week

or so. Maybe by then, she'd have the confidence to believe his love was real. He'd never been a patient person, and this one-sided love was no fun at all, especially as he watched how Meg had escalated her search for Mr. Right. She'd dated one guy after another until he'd begun to think she really did see him as just a pal.

Her date today was with the children's pastor, which didn't really worry Ry, though he probably ought to stop by her apartment and get a report on the date. Pastor Kevin seemed harmless, but just being around Meg could make a guy lose his head. He knew that from experience.

The evening rush-hour traffic was as much of a hassle here in L.A. as it was in Manhattan, though the freeways had more lanes and traffic moved faster. A couple of women in a mystic-blue Beamer kept pace in the lane on his left. He'd noticed the car before he'd noticed the woman on the passenger side. About Meg's age, she held a piece of paper to the window with a phone number on it.

When he didn't break a smile or glance her way again, that should have said he wasn't interested, but the driver moved her car dangerously close to his, and the passenger opened her window to yell an invitation he wouldn't have accepted in his wildest pre-Christian days.

Soon he hoped to have a wedding ring he could hold up to show he was taken. For now, he reached for his black Bible, held it up for her to see and threw her a friendly smile, fully ready to be her brother in the Lord.

His potential new friend flashed a rude little gesture, and her pal, the driver, abruptly changed lanes and zigzagged out of his line of vision. That was fine with him, though he prayed he wouldn't come upon them in a pile of mangled metal.

Those little sports cars didn't stand much of chance in an accident. He wished he could talk Meg into driving something safer.

Meg. There he was thinking about her again. He glanced over at the empty seat beside him and imagined her there as she had been a few nights ago when they drove home from the hospital. He could almost see her in that pretty pink sweater and her pretty, weary smile. If she were with him now, he wouldn't even notice how tired he was after working a thirty-six-hour shift.

Yawning, he rubbed the back of his neck and tried to shake off his exhaustion. This would be a good time to make his daily top-ten list of blessings. In his first week as a

Christian, he'd been taught to do that, and it always made him feel better to focus on the good things of life.

Naturally, these days, every list began with Meg. How had he enjoyed life without her? If something didn't make her happy, it just wasn't worth it.

Beth made the list today for her encouragement about Meg and for admitting she was the one who'd sent the med school applications. He hoped he could make her glad that she'd gone to the trouble.

Third would be little J.T. Ry planned to be the best uncle any little boy ever had. Fourth would be Trey and Isabel for the future they could have in Christ. Fifth would be Dad. They still didn't have much of a relationship, and maybe they couldn't as long as Mom was a holdout.

Mom . . . Just thinking about her made Ry's heart ache. She made the list because he wanted to love her, and there were a lot of years when he hadn't. How sad, that his mother was still trying to please her father, though she had never received his love. Just as sad, she wouldn't accept Ry's love unless he pleased her.

That was one of the great things about being a Christian. When you felt the Lord's unconditional love, there was a new sense of worthiness, a new ability to love because you felt loved yourself.

In the past, there had been some great women, real sweethearts, who'd tried to show him love and be part of his life. He'd felt bad, not being able to love them back, but, praise God, that had changed, and he'd learned to feel God's love before Meg came back into his life. His love for her filled him completely.

She loved him, too. He knew it, and he could hardly wait for her to admit it. From the way she talked, she still saw him as a rebel who couldn't be trusted to be there tomorrow. Why couldn't she trust God enough to trust him?

There he was, dwelling on the negative again when there were more blessings on his list he could think about.

His new partner was a definite blessing. What Hector Gonzales lacked in know-how, he made up for in compassion and empathy. They'd worked together today as if they'd been partners for years, and their shift had been as demanding as any in New York.

There had been the young woman who'd fractured her ribs and clavicle when she was tossed from her horse. She'd been so spunky, Ry knew she'd be riding as soon as she mended.

There had been the two-year-old who got his head stuck between the slats of his grandmother's antique crib. The real patient was Grandma whose blood pressure had gone sky-high from blaming herself.

There had been the diabetic teenager who'd gotten tired of taking care of herself and the man who fell from a construction site onto concrete. There had been the drunk who'd tried to outrun the cops and the semi driver who'd fallen asleep at the wheel.

Being able to help those patients was a blessing, but the real blessing of the day was meeting Dr. Tebalo again.

When they brought in the semi driver, Ry had run into Dr. Tebalo, the man who'd helped Ry when he needed it most. If it weren't for the doc, Ry still might be cleaning the man's pool for a living.

Rebellious, angry with his family, Ry had turned down all college opportunities until Dr. Tebalo connected him to a full-ride football scholarship at UConn. Connecticut was a good school, but its greatest appeal was its distance from L.A. That scholarship meant Ry had no one to answer to but his coach until God came into the picture.

This morning, when Dr. Tebalo asked about Ry's life, Ry found himself confessing that he wanted to do more with his life now that he'd become a Christian, and that he'd applied to the New York med school and the school attached to that very hospital.

That seemed to make Dr. Tebalo's day. He'd told Ry that he was a Christian himself. In his position, he could put in a good word for Ry here.

Blessings like that were pure gold. His family could have helped, but Ry wanted no obligations to them, not when he would never work with them at Brennan Medical.

He would love to tell Meg about his talk with Dr. Tebalo. She would be so happy for him. Darling Meg, his personal cheerleader and precious ally, might give him all the sass a man could handle, but she never let him doubt that she was on his side.

As he walked around the corner of their building and Meg's apartment came into sight, his heart sank. Kevin, the children's pastor, was kissing Meg. Not only that, Kevin was breaking the five-second rule.

A children's pastor should know how to behave. Five seconds was the limit for a date kiss. He ought to know that. More than five seconds gave a fire a chance to flame. Follow it up with more kisses like it, and you were looking at the kind of feeling that belonged to the woman you loved, for the woman who loved you back.

Whatever Pastor Kevin felt for Meg, she did not love him back. She just couldn't.

"Hi, there," he said slow and easy, trying to keep a grip on his temper.

Kevin straightened and looked around, but he kept his arms around Meg. Meg looked like a doe caught in headlights. Good. She shouldn't have let the wrong guy kiss her that way.

"How's it going?" he said, offering his hand to Mr. Wrong with a friendly smile. "You're the children's pastor of my church, aren't you?"

"Yes," Kevin said, snapping into professional mode, letting go of Meg to take Ry's hand. "I'm Pastor Kevin."

Ry smiled inside. Excellent. That had gone well. "I'm Ry Brennan. Meg and I are old friends."

His old friend Meg pulled her cell phone from her purse, checked her caller ID and said, "Excuse me. I need to take this." She backed into her apartment, but left the door open.

"I didn't hear it ring," Kevin said.

"It was on vibrate," Meg replied. "You two go on visiting." She disappeared into her apartment.

Ry almost laughed. She'd made that up. He was sure of it. But that was fine. He could use a few private words with Pastor Kevin. "So what did you two do today?" he asked.

"Meg and I went to Disneyland," Pastor Kevin said, rocking heel to toe, the picture of a happy man.

"Meggy," Ry corrected. "Her friends call her Meggy."

"Oh?" Pastor Kevin nodded his head as if he appreciated that inside information. "Thanks, man, I'll remember that. Do you have any other tips to share?"

Since Kevin asked, Ry thought he might have a few. "You've probably noticed that Meggy is a very independent person. You don't want to choose things for her, no matter what she says."

"Get out! Today, she made me choose the rides, the food, everything. What was that about?" Pastor Kevin looked alarmed.

Kevin seemed like a very nice young man. "It was probably because you're younger than she is," Ry said, feeling only a twinge of conscience. Kevin *was* young. He would recover. "You haven't been to Disneyland as many times, and she wanted you to have a good time."

"I've been there lots of times," Pastor Kevin protested. "I wanted Meg to have a good time."

"Meggy."

"Yeah, Meggy. Thanks. I've got to re-member that."

"And another thing, Meggy really likes it when a guy plays hard to get. Better let her make the next move."

Pastor Kevin looked unsure. "But I want to see her again . . . soon!"

"If you push her, she might put you off."

The man nodded. "She has been doing that. Should I, like, wait for her to call me?"

"Well, if the two of you are meant to be, it will be. You know how important it is to be with the right one."

"Especially for a man in my position," Kevin agreed.

"Especially." Ry was doing Meg a favor, getting rid of this guy.

"This is going to take a while," Meg called from her bedroom doorway. "Thanks for the nice day." She waved and turned to concentrate on her telephone friend.

"The pleasure was all mine, Meggy," Kevin replied.

The way his girl's head snapped at the "Meggy," Ry almost laughed. She might have hurt herself. Lucky for her, a para-medic was close by.

"Give me a call sometime," Pastor Kevin called. He looked to Ry for approval.

Ry gave him a thumbs-up. "I'll just stay

and put in a good word for you," he said, offering his hand again.

"Thanks, man." Pastor Kevin waved as he walked away.

Ry's conscience twinged again.

Lord, bless Kevin and help him find a good woman, a wonderful woman, and let him leave Meg alone.

There. Ry had put in a good word for Kevin. While he was about it, he prayed the same prayer for the rest of those Mr. Right guys. He really couldn't take much more of them. As soon as Meg finished her pretend conversation, they were going to have a conversation for real.

Meg couldn't remember when she'd been this embarrassed. She hadn't meant to let Kevin kiss her like that. He was a sweet guy who would be a wonderful Mr. Right, but the chemistry wasn't there. She'd promised to give love a chance to grow, but how long was it supposed to take?

After four dates, she didn't blame Kevin for testing the waters with that kiss. She'd hoped that a real kiss would make her feel more like a girlfriend and less like a pal. But the butterfly troop sat on the sidelines and waited for the whole thing to end.

She'd felt so uninvolved that she'd peeked

at her watch to see if it wasn't about time for Ry to come home. That's how she happened to catch Ry's furious glare. Ry never got angry, but he was for a moment.

Then, before she could figure out why Ry was so upset, the moment has passed, and Ry was shaking hands with Kevin, the two of them best buddies. Had she imagined that look?

"Almost through with that call?" Ry asked from the living room, as if he knew she was talking to no one.

She walked out of her bedroom, still pretending. "Talk to you later," she said to nobody, ending the call.

"So how was it?" he asked, not too differently than he had after all of her Mr. Right dates.

"We had a nice day," she answered. Hopefully, he was referring to the whole date, not the last minutes.

"How was the kiss?" he asked, ending that hope.

There was something different about Ry today. He seemed more intense, less patient, not his easygoing self. "I'm not sure," she said, not meeting his eyes. It wasn't in her to lie, but she wasn't about to confess that Kevin wasn't in Ry's league when it came to rocking her world.

"You're not sure?"

"Well, I . . . I haven't had a lot to compare it to lately," she stammered evasively.

"Would that help?" He took a step toward her, his eyes locked on hers.

"Would what help?" she repeated breathlessly, watching him take another step closer.

"Comparison."

"Comparison?" she murmured, trying to catch a breath.

"You said you hadn't a lot to compare that kiss with."

Had she said that?

He took another step, closer still, his eyes on hers.

"This is serious business, babe, finding Mr. Right." It felt terribly serious.

"Why don't we establish a baseline — for comparison's sake." He ran one finger down her jaw.

This would be the time to step back if she wanted to keep up the pretense that all she felt was her old crush.

His eyes moved to her lips. "There are all kinds of kisses, Meg."

His lips touched hers lightly, feather soft. She closed her eyes, the better to concentrate on the flood of sensation.

"That kiss said, 'Are you interested?' " he murmured.

That would be a yes. A big yes.

"Now, this one is going to say, 'Where is this going?' " His lips moved on hers just as softly, but with an intensity that made her cling to his shoulders. Wherever they were going, she was along for the trip.

He raised his head, just a bit, just enough to look into her eyes. Whatever he saw there made him catch his breath, and then he was kissing her as if she were his and his alone.

She'd never felt anything like this flood of sweet longing. It was everything she'd ever wanted, everything she'd ever dreamed of — one man to call her own, one love that would last a lifetime, one wonderful . . .

Hold on. Hold on.

What was she doing? If she let this go on, she would lose Ry for sure. She might as well help Ry pack his bags.

Ry would never intentionally break her heart, but neither would he expect her to take this seriously. How could it be, when the whole thing started as a kissing lesson?

It took every bit of her willpower, but she pushed against his chest, breaking the kiss. "Wow!" she said breathlessly. "That was terrific. Fantastic. Woo-hoo!"

Ry grinned happily. "Now, tell me I'm not Mr. Right."

"Let's just say that Pastor Kevin isn't."

Ry threw back his head in a deep satisfied laugh.

If ever there was a sound of victory, that was it. He thought she'd given him her heart, and he'd chalked it up as a win. Wrong. She would not join that long line of women who lost their hearts to Ry Brennan.

"Wouldn't it be great if you were Mr. Right?" she said brightly, reaching for anything that would keep him from knowing how much she wished this were for real.

That wiped the smile off his face. Hurray for her.

Putting on the act of her life, she added, "It's too bad that you're not my type." The color in his face drained. He looked awful.

Why? What was so bad about that comment? It should be exactly what he wanted to hear. They were just words — words to protect their relationship, to make him feel safe, not make him feel as bad as he looked.

Without a word, he turned and walked toward the door.

"Ry?" She didn't want him leaving like this.

He didn't look back. He didn't slow down.

But then, hadn't she known he would do that one day?

Chapter Twelve

He wasn't her type? That phrase had driven Ry crazy for the past week. How could Meg say something so wrong? How could they be any more compatible, to say nothing of the chemistry between them? They shared the same faith, the same values and the same desire for a family. Nobody would ever love Meg more than he would. How was he not her type?

"What's wrong with you, man?" Hector had been giving him concerned looks the whole shift.

Ry shifted position in the passenger seat, embarrassed that Hector had noticed he wasn't himself. "Woman troubles, buddy," Ry confessed.

"What's the matter? Have you got them fighting over which one you take out on Valentine's Day?"

Ry rolled his eyes. In the old days, that might have been the height of his problems.

"No, just one. Meg."

"Meg? Your sister's friend? That dark-haired hottie we saw having lunch with Dr. Beth?"

"That's the one, and don't call her a hottie," Ry grumbled, wishing he'd kept his mouth shut.

"Well, I won't, not if she's your lady. Way to go, man. She's a babe. So what's the problem?"

As long as he'd gone this far, why not spill his guts? He couldn't feel worse. "She says I'm not her 'type.'"

"'Not her type?' That can mean *anything* — a kiss-off or a payback. What did you *do*, man?"

What had he done? Nothing but pour out his heart in those kisses. "I don't know, other than letting her know that she was the one." It felt good to say it out loud.

"Was that when she said you weren't her type?"

Ry nodded, feeling gut-punched all over again.

"And she said that right after you told her that you were in love with her?"

"Well, I don't think I actually said it, but —"

"*Rookie* mistake!" Hector's look said he'd just lost all respect for Ry. "And I thought

251

you were cool, man. Women want the words, partner. They want the words in blood! You gotta say, 'I love you,' and you can't say it just once. It's like Vitamin D. It doesn't store up. You gotta say it every day. You've got to know *that*."

Okay, he knew it theoretically, but he'd never told anyone he loved them. It hadn't even occurred to him that he needed to say it. Hadn't Meg known how he felt when he'd poured his heart into those kisses?

"As I see it, you have two choices," Hector said. "You go to Meg, say the words and —"

"Beg her to forgive me."

"No! You never beg. Women see that as weak." Hector shook his head in amazement. "I can't believe I'm giving you advice on women."

Ry couldn't believe it, either, but he was so desperate, he was ready to listen.

"At this point, you go to her, probably with flowers, and you say, 'I love you.' You may have to dress it up a little more than that. And then you see what happens."

It wouldn't be easy, but Ry could do that.

"That's Choice One."

He had an alternative?

"The other choice is, you save your pride,

forget about Meg and let me introduce you to my little sister."

Ry's mouth twitched, almost smiling for the first time in a week. "It's nice to have a backup plan," he said, "but I think I'll go with the first option."

"Good call. My little sister's only thirteen."

That did get a smile, not real big, but Ry took a deep breath and felt hopeful. Energy flowed through his veins. He had a plan, and everything would be fine. Meg loved him. He knew it. He'd seen it in her eyes, in her fierce loyalty. More than anyone, she was the constant in his life. He could hardly wait to tell her he loved her.

"Ry?" His partner's voice broke into his thoughts. "Did you hear that? We have an MVA at the intersection of San Josita and Judavera."

Ry snapped out of his fog and turned on the emergency lights and siren. It was time to prepare for the worst and pray for the best in whatever waited up ahead.

As they neared the scene and saw that other emergency vehicles had gathered, Ry's heart seemed to stop. A little white convertible with a tan top just like Meg's had been rear-ended and shoved down an embankment. As crushed as that car was, it would be a miracle if the driver was alive.

But it couldn't be Meg's. There were other cars like hers. It couldn't be her.

Dear God, don't let it be her.

Before Hector brought the ambulance to a stop, Ry had the door open and was rushing down the slope, his heart in his throat.

"Hey!" Hector called. "Ry! The gear!"

He shouldn't have left it, especially if he needed it to help the occupants of the convertible. "How many?" he yelled to the police officer closest to the car.

"Just one, and there's no hurry."

He could have sobbed. He knew what that meant.

Getting closer, he could tell the driver was a woman. But the woman was a blonde! Not Meg! Relief almost took him to his knees.

"What's the matter with you, man?" Hector approached, complaining. "Why leave me to haul everything down here?"

"The car . . . it's just like Meg's."

"But it's not her, is it?" The concern in Hector's eyes made Ry swallow hard. He shook his head, and the two of them went to work, doing what they had to do.

What if it had been Meg? Ry's heart ached with the thought. How could he live without her?

"Thanks, Steve, but I'm seeing someone now," Meg said into the phone, turning down his offer for a Valentine's Day dinner. "If you decide that you want to go on *Dream Date*, call me at the office. You would be a terrific contestant."

Meg wondered how many more of these promises she'd have to make before her Mr. Right candidates stopped calling. She could not go out on one more meaningless date, not when the man she loved lived right upstairs.

And she did love Ry. She was tired of denying it, especially to herself. All the doubts she'd ever had about her capacity to love were gone. This yearning to openly love Ry was so strong, she couldn't play the Mr. Right game or pretend that Ry wasn't part of her every breath, every thought.

She hadn't seen him since he left without a word, but her calendar showed that he'd been scheduled to work. Would he stop by when his shift ended? He always did . . . unless he was still upset with her.

"Meg!" Ry's anxious voice and his heavy knock on her door sent her rushing to open it.

She was through with pretending. If he saw that she loved him, he could run for his life or get used to being loved as he'd never been loved before.

When she opened the door, her heart turned over. Ry leaned wearily, one hand on either side of her door, looking so grim that something had to be wrong. "What is it, Ry?"

His eyes were cloudy with heavy emotion. "I thought I'd lost you. There was this car accident. I thought it was you. What if it had been, and I hadn't even told you that I love you? Even if I'm not your type, you're my —"

Meg put her fingers across his lips, silencing the torrent of emotion coming from her guy. "Did you say you love me?"

He looked at her with worried eyes. "Did I forget to say it again? Yes! I love you. And I need you."

She slid her arms around her guy. Of course he needed her. She'd always known that.

"Meg, I want to marry you, have children with you, spend my life with you."

Those were the most beautiful words she'd ever heard, and being held like this was better than she'd ever dreamed.

"You're scaring me, babe. Say something, okay?" He did look scared. That was different. Ry Brennan afraid?

"I just can't believe this is happening," she said. "Two months ago, you weren't in my life, and a week ago, you were giving me dating advice."

"*Bad* advice . . . while I waited for you to wake up and see that I was Mr. Right," he said with a crooked smile. "Remember when I told you that my partner, Doc, quit the day I got back to New York?"

She nodded. His partner left to go to medical school. She remembered because she'd worried that Ry might feel less of himself because his partner had moved on.

"Doc wasn't the only one who quit that day. I did, too. The two of us worked out our notices together."

Meg was speechless with surprise.

"When you called and hinted that you might come to see me out there, I hated pretending that I didn't get the hint, but my SUV was already packed. I couldn't wait to get back out here to you."

"Why didn't you tell me?" She would have loved to have known.

"I wanted to surprise you."

"And you did! But I was so busy denying that what I felt for you was the real thing, I didn't suspect you felt the same way. I thought you came back for your family."

"I did that on New Year's Eve, but, babe,

you're the reason I'm here now. You're my home."

She snuggled her forehead against his neck and prayed.

Thank You, Lord. Thank You for this precious love. Thank You for knowing who was right for me all along. You answered my prayer when I didn't realize You had.

"Ry?" She lifted her head to him.

Ry looked into Meg's face, her beautiful face, now shining with love, and thought his heart would explode. She wasn't turning him down. Everything was going to be all right. "What, sweetheart?"

"When you were giving me kissing lessons —"

"You didn't need any lessons, babe. I was just jealous that you were kissing Kevin."

"Really?" Her bright smile turned him inside out.

"That, and I was tired of waiting to kiss you myself."

"Well, then . . ."

The way she lifted her sweet mouth went straight to the top of his blessings list. Now that she was his, he'd never let her go.

On Easter morning, Ry came home from work, planning to stop in for a good-morning kiss from Meg before getting ready for church. It was going to be the best day. He was caught up on his sleep, the sun was shining and they would celebrate the Risen Lord together for the first time.

Today Meg's ring finger would be heavy. He'd wanted to give her a ring on Valentine's Day, but she'd said she wanted to enjoy being his girlfriend a little while before she became his fiancée.

They'd made a quick trip to Taos so he could get reacquainted with her mom and officially ask for Meg's hand in marriage. It was old-fashioned, but it felt right.

Bless her heart, Phyllis Maguire had given him a real mother's welcome and a beautiful piece of her art. The sculpture was three children at play, a boy and two girls. Ry, Beth and Meg could have posed for it when they were little. But Phyllis said he was to think of it as the grandchildren he and Meg would give her.

Meg had blushed, but he'd hugged Phyllis and promised to do his part to make that come true.

A promise was a promise. If he gave Meg her diamond this morning, then after church, they could go to Vegas, find a chapel and get married. Easter was a perfect day to start their new life together.

He knocked on her door, holding a heavy

vase of pink roses, just like the flowers he brought her the first day he was here.

The door opened, and he heard the sound of her delighted giggle. He loved that sound. Making Meg happy — that was his goal.

"I assume my favorite guy is somewhere behind my favorite pink roses," she said, guiding him to the coffee table, just like she had that first time.

"Please notice the card," he said, setting the vase down carefully. "Since I was a little slow to say 'I love you,' I wrote it once for each of the roses."

"That's a lot of roses."

"That's a lot of 'I love you's'." Ry never thought he would say anything as goofy as that, but she seemed to like it *and* his Easter-morning kiss.

Gorgeous in a pink dress, Meg wore her dark hair swept up off her kissable neck. She'd set a table for two with pink place mats and pink tulips. The room was filled with the delicious aroma of freshly made coffee, bacon and cinnamon French toast. She had learned to make his favorite breakfast. What a sweetheart.

Soon — very soon — maybe even tomorrow, he'd be waking up with her beside him, and breakfast could start with kisses. She turned to dish up the food, and she looked so cute that he couldn't resist putting his arms around her waist and nuzzling her neck.

"Thank you for this Easter breakfast, Meg," he said, his voice morning husky, or maybe because there was a lump in his throat, knowing how much he loved her.

She gave him one wonderful kiss, which in these circumstances, seemed a little stingy. He could have taken a hundred.

"Sit down," she said, her eyes laughing at him. "Your breakfast is getting cold."

He slipped his tiny gift-wrapped box at her place and followed orders, but he couldn't quite keep his eyes off of her. He loved looking at her, and he didn't mind that she knew it. He loved the way she moved in the kitchen, not especially smooth or graceful since neither of them cooked enough to get really good at it, but with joy and enthusiasm like she did everything.

"What's this?" she asked delightedly, sitting down and picking up her present.

The size gave it away. She had to know. Besides, he'd offered to take her shopping for the ring. Since she would be the one wearing it for the rest of her life, he thought she ought to pick it out, but she'd begged off, saying he was better with choices than she was.

"I have a present for you, too," she said. He hadn't noticed it, but there was a little box by his place. "You first, but not until you've eaten breakfast."

He'd never eaten so fast in his life, not that he wanted to open his gift, but because he couldn't wait for her to open hers.

The box he unwrapped was almost too light to hold anything. When he removed the lid and saw the confetti inside, he laughed out loud. It had to be her list of Mr. Right requirements. Leave it to Meg to find a way to package her trust. He leaned over and lifted her chin for a thank-you kiss. "I love it, babe. Now open your gift."

He held his breath as she removed the jewelry store's fancy gift wrap, hoping she would like the two-carat princess-cut diamond set in platinum.

She stared at the ring with shocked delight, then looked at him the same way.

Why didn't she say something? "We can exchange it," he offered immediately.

She looked at him as if he were crazy. "Ry, this is the most perfect ring I've ever seen." She held it out to him. "Will you put it on for me?"

He slid the ring on her finger and sealed it there with a kiss. He would do anything to protect that love, and that included rethinking his dream. If he had to choose between marriage and medical school, marriage had won.

"There's another ring that goes with that one," he said, knowing how curious his girl was. "Want to see it?"

"Can I?"

"Only if we drive to Vegas and put that ring on your finger today," he said hopefully.

She rose from her chair and put her arms around him, raining little kisses over his face. "I'd love that, but I'd like to have my mother at our wedding, and Pete, Sunny and Beth, too."

"I should have thought of that," he said, feeling selfish. What if she wanted one of those big weddings that took a year to plan? He would hate that.

"Why don't we call the church and see how soon we could be married in the garden there?"

Bless her heart. Meg wasn't going to make him wait long at all.

Meg had never been happier in her life. With the top down on her convertible, she drove to the reception for Beth at Brennan Medical Clinic, enjoying the spring breeze blowing through her hair and the dazzle coming from her ring finger. This past month had been one wonderful day after another, all special because she could openly show Ry how dearly she loved him.

Amazingly, Ry, easily the most popular guy she'd ever known, had seemed to soak up that love like a sponge. Now, she could see that his self-sufficient act and womanizing ways were nothing but a cover for how alone he'd really felt and how leery he'd been of rejection.

By this time next month, all that would change. The two of the them would exchange wedding vows in the lovely garden of their church, and Ry would have the security of knowing he'd never be lonely again.

Somehow Ry had managed to get ten consecutive days off work so they could have a honeymoon. The destination of the honeymoon was Ry's surprise. Though she didn't care for surprises, she didn't care where they went as long as she got to be with him for ten straight days.

Beth and Pete would be their attendants. Mom, Sunny, Shay and baby Meggy would be there for her. Ry's dad, Isabel and baby J.T. would be there for Ry. His mother and Trey had declined.

Isabel, however, was showing surprising

courage these days, probably because Ry had led her to the Lord. The baby would have a Christian mommy, and that was better than all the wealth and position Trey could provide.

Meg drove into the clinic parking lot, praying for a good attitude. She wanted to be kind to Trey, Deborah Brennan and the rest of the family. They were going to be her family, too, and, like Ry, she wanted them to know God.

The whole family made a habit of putting Ry down, and he was so easygoing they didn't know how their words cut. To them, Ry would always be the rebel, the maverick, the paramedic who'd gone his own way and didn't want any part of their world. But things would be different now. She would not let them disrespect Ry because he had a mind of his own.

This party, emphasizing Beth's success at completing her residency and the family's pride in her decision to join the clinic, would also emphasize Ry's failure . . . at least in the family's eyes. Meg was happy for Beth, but she would stand up for her guy if she had to.

The spacious lobby with its skylight and atrium was a lovely spot for the party. Meg recognized many of the guests as the same people at the Brennans' New Year's Eve party, though she didn't see Ry or Beth.

"Well, if it isn't little Meggy," Uncle Charlie said, giving her a smacking kiss on the cheek. "What's this I hear about you dragging our boy Ry to the altar?"

Meg cringed, but she put on a bright smile. "I love him, Uncle Charlie. Ry's the best."

"At what? Fixing toilets?" The old man bent over, laughing at his lame joke.

"Don't mind him," Isabel said with an apologetic smile. "He hasn't heard the good news."

"I think he has," Meg said dryly, still feeling the sting of his crude remarks. "Apparently, he's not all that happy about it."

Isabel frowned. "On the contrary, Meg. Everyone is ecstatic."

Meg could hardly believe that. "Everyone?" Would Trey and Deborah Brennan be coming to the wedding now?

"Well, everyone who knows. I think Grandfather Brennan plans to make sure the whole crowd knows after Beth is formally introduced as the newest staff member."

If that were true, Meg thought she'd better find Ry. She ought to be standing beside him when they announced their engagement. Maybe even more of the family would want to attend their wedding.

Meg edged her way toward the staging area. Surely, she would find Beth and Ry there.

"Darling Meggy!" Deborah Brennan threw her thin arms around Meg and bounced up and down like a high school girl who'd just been named Homecoming Queen. "Isn't this the most wonderful day?"

Deborah and her mood swings. Meg wondered how long it would last, but she put on a happy face and agreed. "It is a great day. I'm very proud of Beth."

"And Ry!" Deborah said, as excited as one human being could be. "I'm coming to the wedding, Meggy! So is Trey. Oh, let's have everyone come. I've never been so happy."

Okay, something wasn't right about this, unless Deborah had given her heart to the Lord. Nothing short of that could account for this wild euphoria.

From the corner of her eye, Meg saw Ry's grandfather shuffle out of a nearby office, followed by Ry's father, Beth and Ry. The senior Brennan leaned heavily on a cane, but he smiled broadly as he shook hands with guests on his way to the podium.

Meg waved at Ry, and he headed her way,

a worried look on his face. Now what had his family done?

"Babe," he whispered into her ear, "we need to talk."

That was fine with her, but it looked as if his grandfather was ready to speak. He tapped the microphone to make sure it was on.

Ry slipped his arm around her waist, bent down and said, "I love you, Meg. Please, don't forget it."

As if she could. She leaned against him and smiled. The butterfly troop danced because their guy was so near.

"Ladies and gentlemen," the senior Brennan began, steadying himself with both hands on his cane as the crowd came to a hush.

Dr. James Thomas Brennan, once chief of staff at Cedar Hills Memorial and founder of Brennan Medical Clinic, was still a handsome man at some eighty-odd years. His white hair had thinned, but intelligence shone from his eyes.

"Colleagues, family and friends," he said in a voice that trembled ever so little, "it is with the greatest pride that I introduce to you the prettiest pediatrician my old eyes have ever seen. Please welcome to the staff of Brennan Medical my beloved grand-daughter, Dr. Elizabeth Brennan."

Meg applauded enthusiastically as Beth and her grandfather embraced. Not only was it a big moment for Beth, this new job meant a lot to Meg, too. Finally, after all these years, Beth would have more time for her.

The senior Brennan waved to the crowd, indicating he had more to say. Here it came, Meg thought, the announcement of her engagement to Ry. She squeezed his hand and looked up at him with a heart full of love.

"I have another announcement, too," his grandfather said, looking straight at them. "Come up here, Ry."

Ry smiled, but shook his head, clinging to her hand so tightly it hurt.

"Don't be bashful, Ry. Get on up here."

Short of outright rebellion, Meg didn't know how Ry could resist. She gave him a little shove toward the podium.

"You're not going to like this, Meg," he murmured.

How could he say that? She absolutely loved it that his grandfather was making a point of being proud of Ry. That was long overdue.

His grandfather laid his wrinkled hand on Ry's shoulder and leaned into the mike, saying, "One of these days — and it had better not be too long if I'm going to be around to have the honor — I'll be introducing another Dr. Brennan."

Meg's heart froze. How embarrassing! This took the prize for manipulation. How could Ry stand his ground in the face of this grandstand play?

"My grandson, Rylander Hamilton Brennan, the namesake of the late Dr. Rylander Hamilton, has just been accepted at Southwest Cal Medical School!"

The crowd roared their surprise and approval. Ry's eyes found hers, begging her to understand. Meg forced a smile to let him know she felt as bad as he did about this unfair maneuver. There wasn't much he could do now, being put on the spot like this, but together, they would straighten it out.

His grandfather quieted the crowd. "There's more good news! In a few short years — about the time one of us old-timers will be ready to retire — this young man will need an office, right here at Brennan Medical, in the specialty of his choice."

The cheers and applause began again. The noise was loud, but not as loud as the sound of Meg's heart, pounding at this terrible lie.

Deborah Brennan rushed to Ry's side,

kissing him on both cheeks. His dad, Uncle Charlie, Uncle Al and the rest of the Brennans crowded around Ry, shaking his hand and patting his back, all with the greatest enthusiasm.

Meg could only stare, frozen to the spot.

"Meg," Beth said, touching her shoulder.

"How could they?" Meg gasped. "It's such a lie."

"Actually, Meg, it isn't," Beth said sympathetically.

"But of course it is."

"Meg, Ry was accepted to medical school."

"How could he be accepted unless he applied?"

"He did apply."

He couldn't have. Repeatedly he'd said he wanted no part of being a doctor.

"Isn't this wonderful?" his mother asked, joining them.

"No, it is *not* wonderful," Meg said firmly. Someone had to stand up for Ry. "You will not push Ry into this."

"Oh, Meggy," his mother said, laughing at her, "you don't know my son nearly as well as you think you do."

"I know he doesn't want this!"

"Meg," Beth said softly, "this *is* what Ry wants."

How could Beth say such a thing? Meg

stepped away from both of them, swamped with anger and disbelief. "Ry doesn't want to be a doctor. He loves being a paramedic. It's just what you want for him, all of you."

His mother stiffened. "Young lady, you need to change your attitude. If you're going to be a Brennan, your place is to support my son in the career of his choice."

"I do, but this is not his choice!" She would not let his family railroad Ry into this. "And it wouldn't be mine, that's for sure."

"Well! If you feel that way, why are you wearing Ry's ring on your finger?" Deborah stared at Meg's beautiful diamond. "You don't deserve to wear it."

That was hardly for Deborah to say.

"Mom!" Beth protested.

"Well, she doesn't! If Meggy doesn't realize what an honor it would be for her to be the wife of Dr. Rylander Hamilton Brennan, then she should take that ring off and leave my son alone!"

That was so outrageous, even for Deborah, that Meg had no words to reply. She clenched her teeth and waited for Ry to straighten this out.

He made his way toward her, but slowly, for he was accepting good wishes and shaking hands as if the announcement were real. Could he have taken such a big step without talking to her? She glanced at Beth. Deborah Brennan would say any crazy thing, but not Beth. If Beth knew the truth, she wouldn't lie to Meg.

The sympathy in Beth's eyes sent a chill down Meg's spine. Ry had done this? He had planned a life she wanted no part of? He knew how she felt. She'd just been through it with Beth. Was this how he thought their marriage should begin?

And then he wanted her to live his mother's life . . . and Isabel's? He wanted that for her, too?

His mother was right. If Meg couldn't support Ry's decisions, she shouldn't be wearing his ring. He'd made all these plans without one word to her. What did that say about the two of them making one life?

He'd let her shoot her mouth off, defending him while his mother laughed at her. What kind of love would set her up for this kind of embarrassment? And Beth had been a party to the whole thing. That didn't say much for Beth as a friend.

Meg was so angry with all of them that she tugged at her ring, eager to have it off her finger. She wouldn't be a Brennan if they offered her the moon. Since Ry had included Beth in his big secret, let Beth be the

273

one to give him the ring.

"Here," she said, putting the ring in Beth's hand. "Your mother is right. I don't *deserve* to wear this."

Beth grabbed her arm. "Meg! Don't do this! It's not like you think."

Maybe not, but it was close enough. She glanced at Ry, still busy collecting congratulations. Well, good for him. He'd been in the doghouse with the family long enough. Let the happy celebration continue, but she was out of here. She headed for the door, wiping tears from her eyes.

"Well, little Meggy," Uncle Al said, catching her elbow. "It looks like our boy is going to amount to something after all."

"He has always amounted to something," she said fiercely, shrugging free and moving on. Why couldn't they have seen that and accepted Ry as he was?

Chapter Thirteen

Hemmed in by his family and their colleagues who couldn't wait to welcome him to the fold, Ry struggled to show that Christ's love had changed his life. It was a sham. Rage boiled inside, mostly at himself for telling Beth that he'd received his acceptance letter today.

Before he'd had a chance to tell her the letter made no difference because he wouldn't be going to med school, she was off and running, eager to make Mom happy and Dad proud. Mom was telling everyone while Dad bragged to Grandpa.

Since it was Beth's day, Ry hadn't expected Grandpa to make that premature announcement. His heart almost stopped when he saw the shock on Meg's face. She should not have found out that way, especially when he had no chance to assure her that he would never make a decision like that without her blessing. Being accepted was a dream come true, but he could find another dream a whole lot easier than he could find another Meg. There wasn't another Meg. No one loved him like she did.

What could he have done when Grandpa started that announcement? He could hardly interrupt and say, "Just kidding, folks." Nor could he blurt out the truth and say, "While it is true that I did apply, I was accepted and I would love to go to med school, I won't be going because the woman I love hates the idea."

That would hardly have endeared Meg to the family. They wouldn't understand her perfectly justifiable feelings, but he did. Maybe he could reapply after they were married and Meg felt secure in their marriage. Maybe not. He had to trust the Lord for all that. If God wanted him to be a doctor, it would happen someday.

He shook one hand after another, all the while wondering what he could do to make up for not telling Meg before now. It was his pride that had gotten him into this jam. He'd been so concerned with potential rejection that he hadn't trusted Meg to love him, successful or not. No matter how angry she was about this, he had to remember that he had no real defense.

But Ry knew Meg. One of the darling

things about her was she never stayed mad for long.

She loved pink roses. He'd get her dozens of them, and he would take her on the dream date she described, complete with that boat ride to Catalina, no matter how seasick he'd get. She would forgive him when he apologized and promised that he'd never do anything behind her back again.

When he finally broke free of the well-wishers, he saw his mother and Beth standing where Meg had been. Mom wore a tremulous look of pride, but tears ran down Beth's cheeks. Her eyes begged forgiveness as she held out her hand.

Fear shot through his body. It looked like Meg's ring in Beth's hand, but it couldn't be. Meg wouldn't do that. She wouldn't bolt without giving him a chance to explain.

"Darling," his mother said, "I couldn't be more thrilled! Finally, you're following your destiny!"

Meg was his destiny. "Where did she go?" he asked hoarsely, looking to Beth for a straight answer.

But Beth wouldn't meet his eyes. She just put the ring in his hand. Heavy as a boulder, fear crushed his chest. He closed his eyes, imagining what it must have taken for Meg to leave this way.

"It doesn't matter where Meg went," his mother said spitefully. "She doesn't belong in this family, not after the way she talked to me."

"No," Beth protested firmly. "Ry, that's not what happened." His sister finally had the guts to look at him.

"What's going on here?" his dad asked, joining them.

Ry showed him Meg's ring.

His dad clasped Ry's shoulder in sympathy. "What happened, Beth?"

"When Grandpa announced that Ry was going to be a doctor, Meg thought Ry had been set up, and she stood up for him like always. Mom scolded her and said that Meg didn't deserve to wear Ry's ring."

"Well, she doesn't," his mother snapped.

"Mom! How could you say such a thing!" Ry had been on the receiving end of his mother's venom so often he was practically immune, but Meg wasn't. The thought of her taking his mother's abuse made him so angry he shook.

"Deborah, this time you've gone too far," his dad said in a quiet but intense voice, his face flushed with anger.

"You will not speak to me that way," Deborah snapped imperially.

"It's time someone did. Son, go after

Meg. I'll deal with your mother."

"*Deal* with me?" she shrilled. "No one *deals* with me. I'm the daughter of Dr. Rylander Hamilton!"

Pity blended with rage on her husband's face. Looking at Beth and Ry, he said, "I'm so sorry. I should have done something about your mother long ago."

"Do something about me?" she repeated in rage.

Grasping her elbow, her husband said, "You will not destroy one more person's happiness, Deborah." He moved her through the amazed crowd.

"Let go of me!" she protested wildly, grasping at people to slow their departure.

Uncle Charlie took her other arm. "Settle down, Deborah, or James will have you institutionalized."

"He wouldn't dare!" she screamed. "He can't do that!"

"Actually, Deborah, he can," Uncle Charlie said. "I've waited for years to see you in a psychiatric lockdown unit."

The three of them disappeared down the hall. Ry wouldn't have believed it if he hadn't seen it himself.

"That's something I never thought I'd see," Beth said in awe. "Maybe some good will come of this, Ry."

"But at Meg's expense?" he said bitterly.

"I'm so sorry, Ry. Meg may never forgive me, and you may not, either, but I'll be praying for you both."

Ry headed for his car, thinking how great he would have felt, hearing Beth say that she would be praying, if he wasn't so worried about getting to Meg. Hopefully, she had gone home, and he would find her there.

Meg locked her door, slid the dead bolt into place, pulled the shades and crawled into bed, intending to stay there forever. She couldn't think, couldn't pray, couldn't begin to understand how she could have been so wrong about Ry. Had it been a game for him, making her fall for him, telling her one thing and planning another?

The thought went round in her head, an endless cycle of disillusionment. Nothing made sense, and the hurt went so deep, it might never go away.

She should pray. In times like this, you were supposed to pray and rely on the Lord to work things out. She couldn't even speak her prayer aloud.

Lord . . .

That was as far as she got before the tears took over. Wiping them away, she tried again.

Lord . . . I need Your help. Please, let this

*pain go away. I know that all things work to-
gether for good to those who love You. I'm one of
those who love You. Though I can't see how this
is going to work for my good, it will.*

*Your Word says that You have a plan for my
life, a plan for my good. I'm remembering that
and saying these words in faith, barely believing
them, because my heart feels broken.*

*Show me Your way. Please help Ry and me to
get through this.*

"Meg!" Ry was at her door.

She should have expected that.

"Meg, sweetheart! Open the door!"

Not today.

"Babe, I know you're in there. Please, let
me explain what happened."

They would work out a friendship. But
not today.

The phone rang. She pulled the plug and
turned off her cell phone, as well. Ry kept
calling her name and knocking on the door.

Pretty soon everyone at Los Palmas would
know something was wrong. Hadn't she had
enough embarrassment for one day?

She got up and went to the door. "Ry,"
she said, talking through the door.

"Yes!" He sounded relieved. "We have to
talk, Meg."

"Please leave me alone."

"Babe, open the door. Let me explain —"

"Did you hear what I said, Ry?"

"I can't leave you alone."

"You can if you ever loved me."

"If I ever . . . Meg! You know I love you."

No, she didn't know that.

"Will you call me when you're ready to talk?"

Probably. They would have to get past this. That's what Christians did. They didn't take offense or give it, and they didn't hold a grudge. With God's help, she would get to that point, but not now. She could not bounce into happy acceptance of Ry's secret plans.

"Meg?"

"We'll talk," she said. That was the most she could promise. "Now, will you leave me alone?"

Through the peephole, she watched him run his hands through his hair, frustration and anguish in every move. Strangely, she didn't care. After a lifetime of caring about Ry, of being on his side, of making things better for him, she just wanted out.

One-sided love was too much to bear.

She crawled back into bed and stared at the ceiling, listening for sounds from Ry's apartment, but he was being very quiet, very considerate. Good for him.

Someday this crushing misery would be

just a memory. Someday she would get used to being alone.

Maybe she would get a cat for company. A female cat. A cat wouldn't be any better at returning her love than Ry was, but at least a cat wouldn't give her a dream, then take it away.

Meg ended her call to Pete, glad that she had a brother who didn't ask too many questions. As he had so many times before, Pete had come to her rescue, offering her a hideaway for as long as she liked. Staying with Pete and Sunny would mean a longer commute to work, but it would keep her from running into Ry.

Ry may have surprised her yesterday, but she knew what would come next. He wouldn't let this end without a full-blown, charming explanation and a humble, Christian apology. He would expect her to be understanding, forgiving and totally supportive, just like always.

And why not? Hadn't she always backed him, even when he walked out on people who loved him, like his Grandma Rose? When he went his own way then, she'd believed he had a good reason, and he probably had a good reason now. If Ry wanted to be a doctor, if he felt that was what God wanted of him, he ought to do it. He would be a wonderful doctor.

But she would not be his wonderful wife, waiting for him to show up when he could. That was not her idea of marriage. She would trust God for something better.

Her brother had prayed with her, asking God to give her a sweet spirit. She wanted that, too, but it was hard to feel sweet with this heavy weight in her heart.

She picked up the bags she had packed and prayed she wouldn't run into Ry on the way to her car.

Ry had spent the longest night of his life, waiting in his SUV, knowing that Meg would have to come out of her apartment sometime. He'd never prayed so hard. She had taken a terrible blow, but it would be okay once he got to talk with her. He had to believe that.

The coffee cake twins, who knew everything that happened at Los Palmas, had found him out here in the parking lot. Meg had real friends in those women. They didn't have a clue what the fight was about, but they were on her side and said he should say he was sorry.

He would love to as soon as Meg gave him the chance.

During his nightlong vigil, the twins kept

him supplied with food, coffee and encouragement for the sole purpose, they said, of making sure he was sharp enough to apologize properly. He'd practiced apologies all night and prayed that he would have the right words.

Not long after sunrise, his vigil was rewarded. Meg came out of her apartment, but his relief turned to blazing anger when he saw that she had a piece of luggage over her shoulder, a heavy-looking tote bag in one hand and her big black purse in the other. She was sneaking off without giving him a chance to explain?

When she saw him coming to meet her, her shoulders sagged in defeat. Her pale face was puffy, she hadn't bothered with makeup and she looked as if she didn't have the energy to put one foot in front of the other. She must have had as miserable a night as he'd had, but neither of them would have had to suffer if she'd given him a chance to explain.

Taking both pieces of luggage and her purse, he walked beside her, carrying her things just as he would have if the two of them were off to start a vacation. "Where are we going, babe?"

"It doesn't matter," she said, not meeting his eyes.

It did to him. "Are we going to be gone long?"

"I'm not sure."

After a sleepless night, he might not be at his best, but he was pretty sure he wouldn't have liked this attitude anytime.

She popped the trunk, and he stowed the luggage inside. This was his chance to apologize, and as irritated with her as he was, he needed to do it right.

"Meg, I didn't know that Grandpa was going to announce that stuff about me. I was as surprised as you were."

Her blue eyes were cloudy with misery. "But Beth said it was true. Have you been admitted to medical school?"

"Yes, that part is true, but —"

"Then why keep it such a big secret?"

"Because there was a good chance I wouldn't be accepted. If I didn't get in, I didn't want anybody to know." There, that was the raw truth.

"And I'm 'anybody'?"

"No! You're the woman I love, but a man doesn't want to look bad in his woman's eyes."

Her eyes narrowed. "Here's a clue for you, Ry. A man looks better when he's up-front and honest."

"You're right, but it isn't as bad as you think."

"You told your family, but you didn't tell me."

"That was a very bad mistake, but I can explain."

"You wanted to get married at Easter. What if I'd said okay? Would you have told me before the wedding?"

"I don't know," he said honestly, "because it didn't matter then."

"It didn't matter?" She looked at him with such disgusted amazement that he had to backpedal.

"Let me rephrase that. It would have mattered if I were still planning to go to med school, but I wasn't."

"You had applied, you were worried about being accepted, but you weren't going to go?"

"Put that way, it does sound odd, but it's the truth. Meg, I applied while I was still in New York. Then I saw your reaction to Beth going to med school, and I realized what you thought about being a doctor's wife. I knew you wouldn't want me to go, and I'd given up on the idea by Easter. Believe me, I wouldn't make a decision that big without you being in on it."

"But you let me think you didn't want to be like the rest of your family."

"I don't want to be like them! Long before I fell in love with you, even before I came back here on New Year's Eve, I knew that I wanted to do more for people than I can as a paramedic. But it wasn't until I became a Christian that I let myself admit how much I wanted to be a doctor — not like Mom's father or the family. I wanted to be an ER doc, and I told my dad and Beth as part of my testimony for the Lord, to show them that I wasn't a rebel anymore."

The way her eyes softened, he may have won his case.

"I got my acceptance letter yesterday," he said, so grateful that he'd gotten this chance to explain. "I showed it to Beth and Dad. Then, before I had a chance to say my plans had changed, she was off to tell Mom, and Dad was telling Grandpa. I couldn't get to you to explain before Grandpa made that bogus announcement. I'm so sorry. It shouldn't have happened that way."

She reached out and stroked his cheek. "Don't worry about it. I'm glad for you, Ry."

Her tired eyes met his, and he knew it was going to be okay. He loved her so much, and he would never hurt her again.

"It's wonderful that you'll be part of the family," she said softly. "You'll have a good chance to win them for the Lord, and you'll make a wonderful doctor."

"No, I'll make a wonderful husband."

She shook her head gently. "I don't think the two go together, Ry."

"They don't," he agreed. "That's why I'm not going to med school. I'm not going to risk losing you."

She bit on her bottom lip and looked so unhappy, he knew something was wrong. What had he said? What was so bad about wanting to hold on to the woman he loved?

"You *are* going to medical school, Ry." Her voice was husky with tears.

What was she talking about? He'd just said he wasn't.

"I won't let you give up anything that important for me." He'd never heard such steely determination in his girl's voice.

"But you would give up on us?" She was. He could see it on her face.

"No one should have to sacrifice a dream to be loved, Ry. People can't live with that."

"It's not a sacrifice when there's something else you want more." She had to believe that.

"You can say that now, but later, you would blame me."

"You don't know that, Meg."

"I think I do."

Blood rushed to his head. "So you're

leaving? Whether I go to med school or whether I don't, I lose you?" He could barely get the words out.

"Ry, you're going. And you'll be so busy, you won't notice whether I'm around or not."

She was dumping him. And this was the real reason he'd put off telling her about med school. He had known she would insist that he go if she found out he'd applied. "If you can believe I'd ever be too busy to love you," he said bitterly, "I've got to wonder what your idea of love is."

That struck home. A flash of anger crossed her face, but she pressed her lips together and said nothing.

"And I've got to wonder," he said, so angry he could hardly speak, "if all this hasn't happened for the best."

That definitely hit home. Her blue eyes were dark with fury. "If you think your big surprise was 'for the best,' then maybe it was. Maybe it was part of God's plan for you, Ry."

Just what he needed, a sermon from Meg to validate her throwing their love away. "God has a plan for both of us, Meg — you and me, even if the two of us aren't meant to be."

Chapter Fourteen

On the first Sunday afternoon in June, Meg lay on a chaise on Pete and Sunny's deck, hoping the warm sun on her body would lull her to sleep. She was always tired these days.

If she could sleep, she wouldn't think about Ry lying on this very same chaise five months ago or how it felt, smoothing sunscreen over his shoulders and the tattoo of his grandmother's initials. That was a very sentimental gesture from a very good man.

This Saturday, six days from now, she'd expected to marry that very good man and love him forever. Well, the last part was still true. She would always love Ry.

The rhythmic sound of waves splashing the shore was a peaceful, lulling sound. If she concentrated on that, she wouldn't think about this Saturday and the wedding they'd planned, though it would have been a beautiful wedding. Small, intimate, it was to have been a simple exchange of vows to love each other forever and put God first in their lives.

The setting would have been the lush garden of their church with its landscaped arch and the birds that sang overhead. A harpist would have played sweet worship music while Pete walked her down the aisle. Ry would have been there, waiting with that look that said he just loved what he saw.

She had never expected a man to look at her quite that way, and she never expected to see it again. But how she missed it. She missed his smile, his laugh, the sound of his voice, the touch of his hand. She longed for his kiss, his strong arms around her and the joy of knowing Ry was hers.

Miraculously, he had been hers, if only for a little while. It had been a humbling experience to be loved the way he seemed to love her. He'd called her his "home," and he'd been the man of her dreams.

But they weren't "meant to be." Those were Ry's words, the last he'd said to her a full month ago, and, endlessly, they'd circled in her mind. She'd been so sure that God had put them together. Apparently, she had been wrong.

Even as they planned their wedding, Ry had known he would have to give up his dream so that she could have hers. He must have believed they were "meant to be" then. What had he said? That he would rather be a good husband than be a good doctor? Didn't he know she would never let him do that?

Sometimes she wondered if she would feel this continuous ache of loss if she could hold on to her anger. Her first fury made her numb to the pain. She'd felt such betrayal, with Ry and Beth, both keeping her out of the loop and letting their family in on his plans. For days, she couldn't understand how they could have done that, but prayer had softened her heart.

Beth had only acted with Ry's best interest at heart. That's what a good sister did. Meg had forgiven her even before Beth sent a note, saying she knew Meg needed some distance from the Brennan family, but she would be there whenever Meg needed her.

Meg sent flowers back, but Beth was right. She did need space from anything that reminded her of Ry.

Sometimes Meg still felt a blast of righteous indignation at the way Deborah Brennan ordered her to take off Ry's ring, but how could Meg stay mad at a woman who was under psychiatric care? In her note

Beth said her mother was finally getting the help she'd needed for so long.

Meg wasn't even angry with Ry. Yes, he'd fooled her completely, but she understood his pride as well as his family situation. Of course Ry wanted to please the Brennans. She hadn't been kidding when she told Uncle Charlie that it was time Ry was out of the doghouse, and it was completely admirable that Ry wanted to win them to the Lord.

Without anger, though, all that was left was regret. Deep and painful, regret had a life of its own. Supposedly, people didn't change unless they were motivated by pain. If that were true, her mind was open for whatever God wanted her to see. Did the Lord want her to settle for less than her dream?

If Ry got his dream, he earned a place of respect with his family and the chance to use his God-given gifts. That was exactly what she wanted for him. But if she married Ry, it would be just like her parents' marriage, with each of them following their separate lives.

Medical school was a terrible way to start a marriage. To be sure she wasn't wrong about that, she'd asked around, and everyone agreed that a med student's complete focus was his education. That training went on for years.

"May I join you?" her sister-in-law asked.

Meg patted the chaise beside her, welcoming Sunny's company.

"How are you doing?" Sunny asked with real caring. Sunny had mothered Meg as if she were recovering from major surgery instead of a broken heart.

"Fine," Meg said automatically.

Sunny lifted one brow.

Meg smiled. Sunny was a coach and high school teacher before she had the children, and she still worked with teenagers at church. Not much got past her.

"I was just thinking how a month seemed like such a short time to prepare for our wedding when Ry and I set the date. Now I can hardly wait for the day to be over."

"Six days until Saturday. There's still time to change your mind," Sunny said sweetly.

"About what? Ry was right. We weren't 'meant to be.'"

They lay there, not talking, with only the sound of the waves and a couple of seagulls breaking the silence.

Sunny turned on her side. "Meg, do you mind if I tell you something?"

Meg adjusted her sunglasses. That sounded like the prelude to a lecture, but if anyone has earned the right to speak her mind, Sunny had.

Sunny patted her hand lovingly. "I think we ought to talk about marriage, Meg."

"You don't think your timing is a little off, Sunny?"

"Well, I don't believe we've talked about that."

They hadn't? It seemed as if they'd talked about everything, not only during the past month that she'd stayed here at the beach house, but in the five years since Pete and Sunny met.

"Meg, I know you want a marriage where your husband is your best friend —"

"Like you and Pete."

Sunny looked at her as if Meg were joking. "Meg, you're my best friend more than Pete is."

Meg didn't want to hear that. How could Sunny say such a thing when Pete loved her so? "Is something wrong between you two?" she asked softly, dreading the answer.

"No, not at all! We have a great marriage. I'm as sure of Pete's love as he is of mine. But, living here, you've surely noticed how much he's away on business?"

Meg had been surprised at that. She'd even wondered how Sunny could seem so happy with Pete gone that much.

"Your brother is a wonderful daddy and a good Christian man, but, Meg, his mind is on his work most of the time. I have to admit, there was a time when I resented that."

Meg didn't blame her. That's why Meg's ring finger was bare.

"But then Pastor Tim talked about how our work is our ministry as much as the things we do for the Lord at church. When we think of our work as a way to serve the Lord, there's greater joy in the day and greater contentment in a family."

Meg had no problem with that. She'd been trying to think of her work that way ever since she heard that sermon.

"The way Pete builds houses at modest prices for families is his ministry. My church work with the teens and taking care of Shay and Meggy are my ministries now. I don't expect Pete to be interested in the tiny details of my life any more than I'm all that interested in the tiny details of his, and I don't count on him to meet my every need. I have my best friends for that, and my best friends are you, my neighbor Bev and Cathy from church."

As much as Meg loved hearing herself named as one of Sunny's best friends, she couldn't help feeling bad that her brother was left out. "But what about Pete?"

Sunny's face softened with love. "My darling husband is more than my best friend. He's my best love and the constant in my life. He's my champion and comfort when life seems too hard. I couldn't love him more."

Meg's concern melted. She was so glad her brother had Sunny to love him.

"If our ministries overlapped," Sunny said reflectively, "or if we shared more interests, I suppose we might be true 'best friends.' Some couples are, but I can't imagine them being any happier than Pete and I are."

Meg couldn't argue with that. Their home was filled with love.

"When I think of the military couples who are often forced to spend much of their lives apart, I'm grateful that Pete is at home as much as he is."

Meg got the point. Sunny wasn't terribly subtle. The military couple analogy was a good one. That was the kind of marriage she would have with Ry if he was in medical school.

"Some couples work different shifts," Sunny added, again not very subtle, "and others have to hold down multiple jobs to make ends meet. Don't you think it's the *quality* of the time you share that's important, more than the *quantity?*"

"Why wouldn't a person want both?" Meg asked, not meaning to argue, but that was what she wanted.

"It gets down to what God wants. Sometimes He uses a couple as a pair for His purpose, and they are more powerful together than if they each worked alone. But some couples are so wrapped up in themselves, that they have no ministry. They leave others out, even their children."

Meg's heart turned over, knowing that Sunny was speaking from personal experience about that. Her parents' political ambitions had left Sunny out.

"Then there are couples like Pete and me who have separate giftings and separate ministries. Separately, we touch more lives than if one of us gave up his life to devote to the other's work. God seems to use couples both ways, according to His need."

More than anything, Meg wanted God's will. Could her ideal of marriage be wrong? It had been formed before she'd become a Christian. She'd surrendered many old ideas as she'd realized they were not God's way. Was this one more thing to surrender?

God's plan might not be what she thought she wanted, but she would never know unless she let faith take over.

"You and Ry could work this out, Meg.

It's not too late for you to have your wedding day."

Hope flared in Meg's heart, but fear crowded it out. Choices. She'd never been good about making them, and here she was, faced with one of the biggest in her life.

They sat there quietly, as the waves came and went, an unending testimony to God's control of the universe. Meg thought of the strength of Pete and Sunny's marriage and the happy home her own parents had given her. Did she have to have her way about her future or could she find the faith to build a new dream?

"Should I call Ry?" she wondered out loud.

"What could it hurt?" Sunny answered encouragingly.

"It could hurt a lot if he said again that we weren't 'meant to be.' "

"But Ry said that right after you'd given his ring back. You'd broken his heart, Meg. Those words came from wounded pride. Are you going to let them rob you of your wedding day?"

It was almost midnight on Monday, and Ry had nothing to do but lay on his bunk at Field Medics, waiting for a call to come in. He listened to Hector snore and wondered if Meg's day had been happy. Was she counting off the days to their wedding date as he was, or had she gone on with her life? Maybe she'd even resumed her search for Mr. Right.

How could she do that? He couldn't imagine himself with anyone but her. When he wasn't at work, he hung around his apartment, soaking up memories of her, and listened for any sound that she might have returned. He would never move, not when the place held memories of Meg giving him all the sass he could handle and loving him more than he was worth.

He took her picture from his shirt pocket and held it in his hands. In the darkened room, he couldn't see it, but he didn't need to. Her image was burned into his mind. Holding the picture was just a pitiful way to hold on.

This Saturday, five days from now, his loneliness would have been over. Some guys weren't all that keen about wearing a wedding ring, but Ry had looked forward to it. He'd wanted that symbol of belonging, and he'd loved the idea of taking care of Meg for the rest of his life.

He regretted so many things, like taking so long to tell Meg he loved her — especially when she admitted the Mr. Right search had just been a ruse to hide her feelings for him. He regretted that he would miss the chance to see her walk down the aisle on their wedding day. The dream of that day had kept him going for the month they were engaged. And he felt really bad that he would miss the joy of surprising her with their honeymoon destination.

Surprises were not Meg's thing, but he'd known she would love this one. She'd described the five-star Hawaiian resort where Stan and Tami had their dream date as the most romantic place she'd ever seen — and that was saying something, for Meg had been on plenty of other couples' dream dates.

She'd even shared her daydream of the two of them there, and he'd planned for the whole thing to come true. There would have been moonlight, roses and candlelight on that terrace overlooking the Pacific. He'd bought a tux for himself and a floaty white dress with a scarf for her, just as she'd described, laughing at herself for having such a daydream.

But Ry loved that about her, and he'd loved hearing her talk about watching the paramedics save Stan's life and how proud she was of Ry for doing important work like that.

What would have happened if he had told her right then that he hoped to do work just as important, working as an ER doc? Would he have lost the approval and admiration in her eyes? Or would he be marrying Meg five days from now?

"Ry," Hector murmured sleepily. "Go to sleep, man. You're so sleep deprived you're gonna kill somebody."

"At least I'll have an excuse," Ry said, trying to joke and prove he wasn't as bad off as Hector thought. "What's going to be yours?"

"That I was blinded by the beauty of the woman in the picture my partner holds in his hand like a little girl holds on to her baby doll."

Ry slipped the picture back into his pocket.

"I saw that. Good for you, little buddy."

Ry threw his pillow at his partner as hard as he'd thrown a football in his quarterback days.

"Oof," his partner uttered. Hector rolled over, turned on a table lamp and lobbed the pillow back.

Ry caught it with one hand and tucked it under his head.

"So, how long are you gonna mope?" Hector asked, looking at him with disgust.

"As long as it takes."

"For what?"

"I don't know." If he knew how to pull himself out of this, he would.

"Have you called her yet?"

Ry looked away. Every day Hector asked that. Every day the answer was the same. There wasn't any reason to call. Meg didn't want him, not on his terms, not on hers.

"You're just a sorry case," Hector said with no pity at all for Ry's pain.

That was good. Ry couldn't have taken pity.

"We're off in a couple of hours. How about we get some breakfast or go to the beach or something?"

"Not today."

"You always say that! And then we come back to work, and I ask you what you did, and every time, it's the same thing. 'Nothing.' You're wallowing, man. Like a big old hog, you're just wallowing, and it is not pretty. You've got to move on."

Ry sighed. He would when he could. Grief was a process. Hector ought to know that.

Since it looked like it was up to him to save his partner's love life, Hector went to the TV studio on Tuesday morning.

304

"I'm here to see Meg Maguire," he said to the receptionist, striking a pose, one thumb tucked at the waist of his black leather pants. Hopefully, he looked like a suave *Dream Date* contestant.

"Is she expecting you?" the young woman asked, her gorgeous Latin eyes appreciating the trouble he'd taken to look this good.

"Tell her I'm Ry Brennan's partner." He spoke with more bravado than confidence. He'd taken a chance, showing up like this, but he had to do something. His partner was a mess.

The little cutie talked softly into her phone. The name on her desk said she was Vanessa. He wondered if Vanessa was seeing anyone. Maybe he'd ask her out after he did what he'd come here to do.

Vanessa smiled at him brightly. "You're in. Meg says to send you on back."

He gave her a flirty wink and followed her directions to Meg's office, rehearsing again what he planned to say. He had to get this just right . . . for his own sake as well as his partner's. Working with Ry wasn't fun anymore.

Meg could hardly believe it. Ry's partner was on the way to her office? Vanessa said that Hector Gonzales looked like a perfect

Dream Date candidate, but Meg was more interested in what he could tell her about Ry.

Hurriedly, she slicked on a fresh coat of lip gloss and fluffed up her hair. If Hector took a report back to Ry on how she was handling their breakup, she had just enough pride to care about what he would say.

She ought to look knee-deep in work. That shouldn't be hard, not with the tall stack of contestant applications on her desk. She's never been so behind in her work, but her heart wasn't into matching couples. She needed a new job, something that didn't focus on people looking for love. When she'd made such a botch of her own love life, what right did she have, interfering with others'?

She'd taken Sunny's advice and called Ry, twice each on his home phone and his cell. Each time, she'd gotten his voice mail and hung up without leaving a message. What kind of message could she have left?

"Hi, just calling to ask if I can have my ring back."

That would have been brilliant.

"Hey, Ry! The wedding's still on. See you there."

That would have been just as bad.

Four more days until Saturday. Unless a

miracle happened, it would be the worst day of her life. But Monday would roll around, and she would look for a new job and a new apartment, too.

She couldn't live at Los Palmas where she risked running into Ry any time, any day. Even if he moved away, there were too many memories for her to stay.

Maybe he'd already moved. He wasn't as slow to move on as she was. He would probably go on their honeymoon and call it a celebration from his narrow escape from the marriage that wasn't "meant to be."

The sting of those words hurt every time and brought on a fresh batch of tears. She really had to stop looping that phrase. Grabbing a tissue, she dabbed at her eyes.

"Meg?" Hector walked through the open door and held out his hand. "Thanks for seeing me."

"No problem," she said brightly, hiding the tissue. "Ry said you would be a perfect *Dream Date* contestant. I thought he'd be perfect, too, and tried to get him on the show, but —"

"Why would you do that?" Hector interrupted, frowning. "He was in love with you."

That took her breath. "But that was back in February. I didn't know then."

"You didn't? I knew the first week we were partners."

"He told you?"

"He didn't have to. It was written all over his face."

Then she hadn't imagined that look.

"He's still crazy in love with you, Meg. I don't know what he said or did to make you so mad —"

"I'm not mad."

"You aren't?" His eyes widened. "Then why aren't you two together?"

It was embarrassing to explain, but maybe God had given her this chance to let Ry know she hadn't factored in faith when she clung to her dream. "I was upset when I found out Ry planned to go to med school, and —"

"Ry's not going to med school!" Hector said as if he knew it for sure.

Had Ry kept his secret from Hector, too? "He didn't tell you about it?"

"No, he told me. But he's not going. It's like he's trying to prove something."

Meg's heart sank. It would be just like Ry to sabotage his own dream.

"I sure wish somebody could talk to him about that," Hector said meaningfully.

For the first time in ages, the butterfly troop stirred.

"Though it probably wouldn't do any good." He shook his head sadly.

"Why not?" She touched her stomach, quieting the troop.

"Well, you know the guy better than me, but I've never seen Ry get talked into anything he didn't want to do."

That was so true.

"I've got an idea!" Hector said with such a sly look that she almost smiled. He'd come here with that idea.

"Why don't you give me a *Dream Date* application? I'll get Ry to help me fill it out. I'll say I saw you, and that you said . . . What should I tell him, Meg?" His eyes dared her to be open and honest.

She took a deep breath. "Tell him I said I was wrong."

Hector rolled his eyes. "Can't you make it something else? Ry won't believe that. Women never admit they're wrong."

"This woman does."

It was a dreary Wednesday morning, perfect weather for Ry's mood. He sat in the Field Medics kitchen, drinking yet another cup of black coffee, so tired he could hardly think. It felt as if his heart wasn't even there in his chest anymore, just a heavy stone that took all the space.

Hector came bouncing into the kitchen and slapped a paper down on the lunch table. "There you go, man. That's your ticket back into your girl's heart."

Ry was in no mood for this kid's nonsense. He picked up the paper and slid it into the waste can.

"Man! You are one self-destructive dude!" Hector fished the application out of the can and slapped it back on the table. "Look at it, Ry! It's a *Dream Date* application. Meg Maguire personally initialed this form to be directed to her attention. It's for me, not you, but I'm going to let you use it. You fill it out nice, take it to the studio yourself and she'll see you."

Ry sighed. "Now, why would I want to do that?"

"Because she said to tell you she was wrong."

"Sure, she did." Ry would believe that when they invented a cure for the common cold.

"Ry, I'm not kidding. I asked her if she wanted me to tell you anything, and that's what she said."

"That she was wrong," Ry repeated, considering it for a moment. No, Meg wouldn't have said that.

"Would I lie? This is a way for you to save

310

face, man. Fill the form out. Pretend that you want to go on her show. If she seems glad about that, you can find an excuse not to actually go on the show. But if she's upset that you want to go on that show, you'll know she wants you herself. What do you have to lose?"

Actually, not much. His pride was all gone.

Wednesday had been a very long day, and this morning had dragged by, as well. Of course it was only two days ago that Hector had shown up here at her office, but she'd believed he would take her message to Ry right away. If Ry still loved her, wouldn't he have called?

Maybe Sunny was right, and Ry wouldn't risk rejection again.

Her phone rang, and she couldn't grab it fast enough. But it was only Vanessa, the receptionist.

"Meg, one of your adorable hunks just dropped off a completed application form for *Dream Date*."

There was nothing unusual about that. "Just drop it in my mailbox, Vanessa."

"It has your initials in the upper left-hand corner of the envelope. You always want those right away."

She'd initialed the application Hector had taken to Ry. "Is the guy still there?"

"No, he seemed in a hurry when he dropped it off."

"Was it the guy who was here Tuesday?"

"Meg, there were lots of guys here Tuesday."

"I'm talking about Hector Gonzales."

"What did he look like?"

"Dark hair, dark eyes, about five foot nine?"

"Hmm, I don't remember him, but the guy that dropped off the envelope has dark blond hair. He was about six feet tall, lean but muscular and he had great dimples when he smiled. He was really cute, Meg."

That was Ry. It had to be. Had he brought Hector's application, hoping he would see her? "I'll come get the form," she said, eager to see if Hector had included a message about Ry. Racing to reception, she wished Ry had waited.

"Wow, you got here fast," Vanessa said, handing over the envelope.

It didn't seem like it. Meg's hands trembled as she tore open the envelope and began reading the application on her way back to her office.

It wasn't what she expected. Ry had used Hector's application, supplying his own name, pertinent data and list of favorites, which matched hers exactly, just as they had in that Mexican restaurant the night his nephew was born.

On the second page, where he was asked to describe his idea of a perfect date, he'd written the one she'd talked about. It was all there — worshiping at church, taking the boat to Catalina, strolling past shops, eating ice-cream cones, dinner at a beachfront restaurant, listening to the waves, watching the stars and taking the last boat back — every last detail. Ry Brennan did indeed have the best memory of anyone she knew.

This very smart man knew her job was to find contestants who might match his answers. He was saying that she was his perfect match.

The butterfly troop flew into action, hunting balloons and confetti. Their guy still loved her, and her knees felt so weak, she had to sit down.

Under "Immediate Plans," Ry had written, "Make up with my best friend." Under "Future Plans" . . . Meg stopped and just sobbed, for Ry had written, "Marry my best friend."

Penned in the bottom margin was the scripture, "Faith is the confidence that what we hope for is going to happen. It is the evidence of things we cannot see. Hebrews 11:1."

How she wished Ry had stayed. She would give anything if she could be in his arms right this moment.

A tap just outside her open doorway made her look up. A bouquet of pink roses came through the doorway, and then Ry peeked his head in. There was such an uncertain look in his eyes, as if he wasn't sure of his welcome, that she couldn't stand it.

Scrambling out of her chair, she rushed to him, her arms open wide. He swept her up in his arms and held her against him, burying his face in her neck. She would rather have two minutes with this man than twenty-four hours a day, seven days a week with any other man.

"I've missed you," he said in that buttery baritone that made the troop twirl.

"Well, you don't have to anymore," she murmured, planting kisses in each darling dimple. "Not if you take it back that we're not 'meant to be.' "

"Did I say that?" Ry grinned sheepishly. "Sweetheart, that was just pride talking. We were always meant to be. Beth believes it so much that she's given her heart to the Lord. She's a Christian, Meg."

Meg's happiness went over the top. She

couldn't wait to talk to Beth. But first, there had to be a serious talk with her guy. She took the roses and laid them on the desk so she could take both of his hands in hers.

"What's this I hear about you not going to med school?" she said sternly.

"I'm not," he said firmly while his eyes roamed her face as if he just loved what he saw.

It wasn't easy, being stern with Ry, when he looked at her with such love. The butterfly troop responded with fluttery flair.

But she had to do this. "Ry, we've had the conversation before, but this time there has to be a better ending."

"You mean, you have to win," he said, teasing.

"No." She didn't mean that at all. "We both have to win."

He wanted that, too, but he'd thought about this for hours. He couldn't see a good life for Meg if he did what he wanted. "I can't go, babe. You lose too much."

"If you don't go, we both lose more."

Ry saw such faith in her beautiful eyes that it took his breath. His darling Meg loved him for better or worse.

"When I was so against the whole doctor thing," she explained earnestly, "I was leaving God out of the equation. Isn't that amazing that I could forget something so essential? Ry, we'll be fine if we follow God's lead."

For weeks now, he had prayed that Meg would trust God enough to trust him. If this was the answer to his prayer, it was sure worth the wait.

"So, we agree?" she asked as if he had no choice at all.

When had Power Woman become so ready to make powerful choices? That had to have come from above.

"I only want God's best for you," he said, loving her so.

Those blue eyes sparkled with mischief. "If you really want the best for me . . ."

"I do," he said firmly, backing that pledge with a kiss, the kind that said he would love her forever.

"Then you'll have to say that again," she murmured, barely breaking that kiss.

"Say what?" It was hard to pay attention when his girl was so very good at this.

" 'I do.' You'll have to say that again on Saturday. In the church garden. With the birds, the harp, the whole thing. That's what would be best for me."

"You didn't cancel our wedding?" he said, almost shouting for joy.

"I couldn't."

"I couldn't cancel the honeymoon, either!"

"Were you planning to go by yourself?"

"Were you going to eat our wedding cake by yourself?"

"Maybe," she said guiltily. "I eat a lot when I'm depressed, and I do love wedding cake."

"We'll take the leftovers on our honeymoon." She could have all the cake she wanted, but she wouldn't be depressed, not if he could help it.

She took his face in her hands and looked at him with so much love, he could barely breathe. He reached for the ring he'd put in his pocket when he knew he was coming here today. "Shall we put this back where it belongs?" he asked, his voice husky with emotion.

She held out her hand. He slid the ring back to its home and kissed it in place.

Meg clutched at her stomach.

"What's wrong, Meg? Are you sick?"

She shook her head. Laughing, she patted her stomach. "Ry, I think it's time you met your dear friends, the butterfly troop."

Epilogue

Five Years Later

A new group of medical students entered the ER of L.A. Medical Center, their eyes wide at the frantic activity. A patient on a gurney moaned as paramedics rattled off her vitals. A white-haired gentleman called for his mommy, and a gunshot teen yelled his head off because the bullet had messed up his new tattoo.

The new redheaded nurse flirted outrageously with the new ER doc, who dismissed her with a look that said he didn't allow that kind of nonsense. If she hadn't been new, she would have known better.

All the ER regulars knew this doc was a one-woman man who took his work seriously and was amazingly competent for a first-year resident. Of course that didn't surprise Hector at all. His old partner was exceptionally smart. If Hector were the one showing up here in need of treatment, he would ask for Dr. Ry Brennan by name.

"Hector!" the doc called. "I need a nurse here."

Hector smiled. It was cool, working with Ry again. He took his place beside Ry, putting his new nursing skills to work, thinking that the two of them still made a great team.

If it weren't for Ry believing in him, Hector wouldn't be here, doing this work. Sometimes he thought about the paycheck he would have earned if he'd become a firefighter or police officer, but he went home every day, feeling as if he'd made a difference. He liked working here.

"Can you watch this patient?" Ry said, glancing at his watch anxiously. "I've got to check on someone."

Hector grinned. He understood. "Tell someone I said 'hi.'"

Ry smiled and took off in a slow jog.

The redheaded nurse frowned. "Where does Dr. Brennan go when he disappears like that?"

"Like he said, he's checking on someone," Hector said, smiling to himself.

He could have said that the doc had a habit of stealing kisses from the media director just down the corridor. The woman's

ID badge read Meg Brennan, and the child she carried under her heart would be born any day to a daddy with an M.D. after his name.

Dear Reader,

This book is dedicated to the man of my dreams. He is my rock, my strength and the greatest blessing of my life. When we fell in love, he said we would have fights, but I couldn't even imagine it. I thought we would share everything, but it turned out that I didn't want to fish any more than he wanted to shop. When he wasn't interested in my every thought and feeling, I felt lonely. When our values and wants did not match, I wondered if I'd made a mistake. The man was not my best friend, and he didn't need me to be his.

Are you nodding your head in understanding or shaking your head at my stupidity? Either is fine. I have shared my youthful misunderstanding for two reasons:

One — if your marriage is not what you thought it would be and you're praying for an answer, maybe it's to appreciate what you have and find a new best friend, maybe someone from church. Live each day with love and laughter.

Two — if you're looking for Mr. Right, he may be closer than you think, but not as perfect as you dreamed. If he's a good man, it may be your joy to love him forever.

My husband just came into the room. I said, "Listen to what I just wrote." He was glad to and sat down, looking outside at a foursome on the golf course. I had just read, "He is my rock, my strength and the greatest blessing of my life," when he jumped up and exclaimed, "Nice shot!"

That's the way we are. I want to talk about life. My guy wants to live it. What do we have in common? Only our family, our friends, our church . . . and our best friend . . . Jesus. It is more than enough. So much more.

Please visit my Web site, www.pattmarr.com, and e-mail me from there or write to me at P.O. Box 13, Silvis, IL 61282. Hearing from you is such an encouragement.

In Him,

Patt Marr

About the Author

Patt Marr has a friend who says she reminds him of a car that's either zooming along in the fast lane or sitting on the shoulder, out of gas. Her family says he's dead right.

At age twenty, she had a B.S. in business education, a handsome, good-hearted husband and a sweet baby girl. Since then, Patt has had a precious baby boy, earned an M.A. in counseling, worked a lifetime as a high school educator, cooked big meals for friends, attended a zillion basketball games where her husband coached and her son played and enjoyed many years of church music, children's ministries, drama and television production — often working with her grown-up daughter.

During downtime, Patt reads romance, eats too many carbs, watches too many movies and sleeps way too little. She's been blessed with terrific children-in-law, two darling granddaughters, two loving grandsons, many wonderful friends, a great church and a chance to write love stories about people who love God as much as she does.

The employees of Thorndike Press hope you have enjoyed this Large Print book. All our Thorndike and Wheeler Large Print titles are designed for easy reading, and all our books are made to last. Other Thorndike Press Large Print books are available at your library, through selected bookstores, or directly from us.

For information about titles, please call:

(800) 223-1244

or visit our Web site at:

www.gale.com/thorndike
www.gale.com/wheeler

To share your comments, please write:

Publisher
Thorndike Press
295 Kennedy Memorial Drive
Waterville, ME 04901